PRATCHETT'S WOMEN

UNAUTHORISED ESSAYS ON THE FEMALE
CHARACTERS OF THE DISCWORLD

TANSY RAYNER ROBERTS

CONTENTS

Fair warning: Here be SPOILERS!   v

1. The Boobs, The Bad and the Broomsticks   1
2. Slash! Stab! A Lesson in Practical Queening.   11
3. Werewolf Glamour & the Sexing of Dwarves   18
4. His Henpecked Voice   29
5. A Wonderful Personality and Good Hair   37
6. The Seamstress Redemption   47
7. Has Scythe, Will Teach School   54
8. Pole Dancers, Goblin Girls, and the Family Man   65
9. The Truth Has Got Her Boots On   73
10. Socks, Lies, and the Monstrous Regiment   79

Also by Tansy Rayner Roberts   93
Sheep Might Fly   95
Love & Romanpunk   97

FAIR WARNING: HERE BE SPOILERS!

1
THE BOOBS, THE BAD AND THE BROOMSTICKS

The Colour of Magic (1983)

The Light Fantastic (1986)

Equal Rites (1987)

Mort (1987)

Sourcery (1988)

Wyrd Sisters (1988)

Pyramids (1989)

Guards! Guards! (1989)

Eric (1990)

Moving Pictures (1990)

TERRY PRATCHETT IS one of those writers that you can see noticeably improving and honing his craft as he goes. One of the aspects of his writing that improved massively over the years was his treatment of female characters, and I always meant to stop at some point to figure out exactly how it was that his portrayal of women changed and developed over several decades.

I started reading the Discworld books in the early 90s, when *Small Gods* (1992) was the latest release. This meant that I read all the books before that in (mostly) the wrong order, and all of the books after that in (mostly) the right order. So it took me some time to figure out what was going on with Pratchett's women, and to wrap my head around the chronology.

The first ten books of the Discworld series are problematic in their portrayal of female characters, particularly the younger women. I certainly don't think this was intentional on Pratchett's part, but an unfortunate result of the fact that in these early books he was largely parodying fantasy worlds and tropes, and only just beginning to develop the Discworld into something more substantial and complex. You can certainly see from his novels that Pratchett was very much aware of some of the dreadful sexism in his source material, and that he often wrote female characters in direct response to problems he saw in the fantasy genre.

His apparent intentions to point out the silliness of the portrayal of women in fantasy, sadly, often backfired.

In these early Discworld books, we find Pratchett mocking the semi-clad, bosomy fantasy women who traditionally reward the handsome hero with their sexy selves. He does this at first by creating semi-clad, bosomy fantasy women who a) say bitchy things to the (not handsome) hero in the hopes that no one will notice they are still a cliché of the genre and/or b) amusingly fail to fall in love with the protagonist but instead reward a less obvious male character with their sexy selves. Examples of this phenomenon include Bethan in *The Light Fantastic*, the glamorous priestess who is cross about being rescued from a temple and chooses to hook up with the aged Cohen the Barbarian instead of giving Rincewind a second look; Conina in *Sourcery*, the glamorous warrior woman who chooses to hook up with the nerdy Nijel instead of giving Rincewind a second look; Ptraci in *Pyramids*, who is totally hot for Teppic and vice versa, until they discover they are siblings and he promptly hands her an empire and his best friend; Princess Keli in *Mort* who goes for the dweeby wizard (finally a hot girl with a taste for wizards, as long as they're not the protagonist!) over Mort; and finally Ginger of *Moving Pictures* and Ysabell of *Mort*, who are constantly bitchy to their respective guys, but ultimately choose them. Oh and don't forget Elenor of Tsort in *Eric*, a parody of Helen of Troy... the joke being that ten years of being a wife and mother will turn the most beautiful woman in the world into someone plump, ordinary and unworthy of a teenager's sexual fantasies.

I should admit at this point that when I was fourteen and reading the Discworld novels for the first time, I adored Conina and Ptraci and Ginger and totally wanted to be just like them when I grew up. I look back on that now and shudder, just a bit. Teenage self, how about we aspire to be something other than a Josh Kirby cartoon character?

And oh, Josh Kirby. There's that, too. Even when the writing in the Discworld books challenged and questioned the roles of female characters in fantasy, the original covers reinforced the clichés so hard that the boobs of the heroines could be classified as lethal weapons in their own right.

Pratchett writes a lovely paragraph in *The Light Fantastic* (1986), only his second Discworld novel, in which he describes Herrena the Henna-Haired Harridan, a barbarian warrior. He expands at length about how in other fantasy worlds she would be dressed in a lurid but impractical costume, but in fact she is wearing some quite sensible armour. *Have a cold shower, chaps, the woman is appropriately attired.*

This elegant and witty piece writing is completely sabotaged by the fact that the cover art, as with all Discworld covers for the first couple of decades, depicts Herrena bursting out of a tiny postage stamp bikini with enormous beach ball bosoms. This is a character who only appears for a page or two in the entire novel, and thus can only have been included on the cover in order to raise the number of scantily-clad breasts to four.

Sadly, that is what I see now when I look back on my favourite Discworld heroines of my teen years—good intentions that simply didn't go far enough. The girls got to look pretty and say the occasional witty line, but they didn't get personalities that ran deeper than their bra size. (Also, it has to be said, they all pretty much had the SAME personality, which was Difficult+Snarky+Beautiful.)

There are some exceptions. Lady Sybil, in *Guards Guards* (1989), is an unusual romantic interest in that she has a fully defined personality, gets lots of witty lines that aren't mean, and is an equal match for the protagonist, Commander Vimes. She's also a woman of mature years who is not lithe and pretty, and thus escapes much of the usual 'I am standing here in my fur bikini being ironic about the sexist portrayal of women' depictions of early Discworld women.

She was developed more substantially later on, but this was a good start.

Then there are the witches. After two books featuring the same hapless wizard running away from trouble and occasionally colliding with astoundingly sexy women who don't want to sleep with him, Pratchett turned his attention to feminist issues with *Equal Rites* (1987). This book tackled one of the most problematic ideas with which he had saddled his Discworld: that magic was segregated by gender, men becoming wizards and women becoming witches, with drastically different magical traditions. In *Equal Rites*, a girl is born with the magic and destiny of a wizard, and with the help of her mentor witch Granny Weatherwax, fights the system to be allowed into the Unseen University instead of simply settling for being a witch.

My teenage self hated this book.

Which is bizarre, because it sounds exactly like my sort of thing. But I think we've already established that there is a big difference between my teenage self's reading tastes and my own.

The problem was that my teenage self was reading through the backlist of Discworld books in the wrong order, and having read the blurbs, I had completely fallen in love with the concept of *Equal Rites*. So I saved it for last. By the time I got to it, my expectations were through the roof, and I resented that it was not the book I thought it was going to be: it was about a child, not a teenage girl or adult woman (yep the fact that it wasn't Conina-Ptraci-Ginger in a wizard's hat seemed like a flaw to me at the time), and while the best thing about the book is indeed Granny Weatherwax, I'd already read her being far more awesome elsewhere. She seemed a pale shade of herself without Nanny Ogg or Magrat to grate against. I later revisited *Equal Rites* more than once, and came to terms with it, though I never learned to love it. Still, it hardly matters now that it is the least interesting book that Pratchett ever wrote about witches. (It's #3 in a series of over 40 books, so that's good news. He got *better*.)

Despite my lack of love for *Equal Rites*, I was disappointed over the years that we never returned to Esk's story. No matter how many times we visited the Unseen University, she wasn't there. We never saw how she turned out, and never got to see her as an adult. Until, of course, the Tiffany Aching book, *I Shall Wear Midnight* (2010), which also features cameos from Nanny Ogg and Magrat. *I Shall Wear Midnight* felt like a satisfying line was being drawn under the saga of the Lancre witches, and having that unexpectedly delightful resolution about Esk made me want to go back and revisit the other witches stories, from the beginning.

Thanks to the wonder of unabridged audiobooks, I reintroduced myself to *Wyrd Sisters* (1988), and immersed myself utterly in what is still, I believe, one of Pratchett's most effective standalone books. You can praise *Reaper Man* and *Small Gods* all you like; I'll take a Witches book over those two every time. Finally, Pratchett stopped satirising fantasy and looked further afield for material to poke sticks at... and he decided Shakespeare would be his first port of call! This glorious work amalgamates the best and worst aspects of the plots of *Hamlet* and *Macbeth*, producing one of my favourite fictional double acts of all time: Granny Weatherwax and Nanny Ogg. Also, for the first time, Pratchett created a young female character (Magrat) with the same ruthless, complicated comedic touch that he brought to Rincewind, Mort and his other male protagonists.

Magrat isn't a sexy treasure with which to reward the hero (or someone other than the hero). She's a real person, warts and all, and her voice is every bit as compelling and sympathetic as it is nasal and long-suffering.

The three Lancre Witches, maiden, mother and crone, (listen to them argue about which is which!) are a masterful creation. It doesn't matter what the plot is, any excuse to see them riff off each other, poke holes in the pomposity of the world and then save it anyway, is a genuine pleasure. The surprise in coming back to *Wyrd Sisters* is just how good the plot is—how cleverly the Shakespearian elements weave together, into an elaborate comedy of errors. Indeed, all of the Lancre Witch novel plots tend to be about stories, and how stories work in a world of magic. This meta-element raises them into being far more than amusing romps with complicated sentences (which I think is a fair description of all the Discworld books before *Wyrd Sisters*).

These are stories about witches who know that fairy tales exist; witches who know about the dangers of cackling too much and getting a reputation for gingerbread houses. *Wyrd Sisters* is about what happens when the legends and stories about witches are used against them as a weapon; and how they fight back. It was fascinating to reread this one so soon after reading *I Shall Wear Midnight*, because there are huge parallels between the plots of the two books, another reason why I thought at the time that Pratchett had deliberately written it as his last witch book, tying up the last remaining threads of the characters.

But back to *Wyrd Sisters*! The female characters are absolutely in command here, on both sides of the story—the Duchess is a magnificently awful villain, one in a long line of marvellous female antagonists set against Granny Weatherwax. She completely overshadows her husband, as is appropriate considering the parallels to Lady Macbeth.

I also want to mention that there are some fantastic male characters in this book. Pratchett writes interesting and complex male characters who work against the traditions of masculine fantasy heroes, the most obvious early examples being Rincewind, Mort and Vimes. One who often gets forgotten about, however, is the Fool in *Wyrd Sisters*.

Everyone else in the story is taking part in a comedy, up to and including the ghost of the dead king, but the Fool is in a tragedy, carrying an abusive past and a more recent emotional burden along with his unwavering, committed loyalty to Duke Felmet, the villain of the piece. Even when he's being funny—and he is very funny—he's utterly miserable. The romance between Magrat and the Fool, with its many wrong turns and awkward silences, is one of the most egalitarian and sincere love stories I have come across in fantasy fiction.

On the other side of the scale, Tomjon is a great creation, and I like what Pratchett says about destiny and kings through his character—for all this story is mostly about Shakespeare's stories, it also nicely undercuts some of the sillier notions of fantasy fiction, notably the legend of the lost king turning out to be exactly what his kingdom needs despite no actual training, a trope that Pratchett also plays with to great effect in the City Watch books. The relationship between Tomjon and his sidekick, the playwriting dwarf Hwel, is a pleasure to read.

Ultimately, the best thing about this book is that triad of witches: Granny Weatherwax, Nanny Ogg and Magrat Garlick, each vibrant characters that leave the rest in the shade. The scene in which the three of them perform a huge feat of magic, recharging broomsticks and flying around the kingdom to transport it in time, is epic and breathtaking—though any scene with the three of them in it makes me happy, even if they're talking about cups of tea and what kind of sandwiches they like best.

After my *Wyrd Sisters* reread, I moved straight on to *Witches Abroad* (1991), which has always been one of my favourites: this is the Discworld novel which most effectively deals with the role of the witch in stories and fairytales, and is pure Ogg-Weatherwax-Magrat hilarity from beginning to end.

Only when listening to Nigel Planer read the unabridged book did I realise something I had never entirely noticed before: this is a fantasy novel in which all the important characters are women.

This is a fantasy novel by a bestselling male author in which all the important characters are women.

We have the trio of Granny Weatherwax, Nanny Ogg and Magrat, travelling to foreign parts. We have the witches/cooks of Genua: Lilith, Mrs Pleasant, and Mrs Gogol. We have Emberella, the hub around which the story is constructed. But the only male characters of any note are a) a frog turned into a prince who rarely speaks and is basically a MacGuffin, b) a cat-turned-human who has no agency, barely any voice, and no personal needs beyond a bowl of fish-heads, c) a zombie, and, d) a dwarf one-note-joke about Casanova, who arrives in the final act and provides some brief comic relief. (Casanunda becomes a far more important character in later books, but is blink-or-you'll-miss-him here.)

How rare is it to find a book that does this? How rare to have a story with so many women in it that you don't even need a romance because the women already have plenty to do? *In the fantasy genre*. This revelation completely did my head in, forcing me to re-evaluate a novel that I had already loved for half my life.

Despite the glamour girls and snarky wenches which populate the first decade of Discworld, the witch books redeem this period for me as a feminist reader. They are packed with female protagonists who are as three dimensional, complicated, flawed and fascinating as Pratchett's best male protagonists, and are allowed to be more important than the men in their stories.

But that's not the good news. The good news is that after this, Terry Pratchett only got better at writing women—and in particular, at writing young women who had a soul as well as (or even instead of) a great rack. There was Angua, Cheery, Agnes/Perdita, Susan Sto Helit and Sacharissa Cripslock. There was even another book that featured all female protagonists (and no witches)…but I'll get to that eventually.

2
SLASH! STAB! A LESSON IN PRACTICAL QUEENING.

Lords & Ladies (1992)

This is the best kind of fantasy novel.

The greatest thing that fantasy as a genre can do is to say something important about our world and history, ideally while also commenting in some way on the traditions of the genre itself, and being a damn good read to boot. If you add to that a bunch of female characters driving the plot, my heart will certainly be won over.

Oh, yes. *Lords and Ladies* is that good.

In one sense, this book is the last third of an unofficial trilogy (with *Wyrd Sisters* and *Witches Abroad*) featuring the original trio of Pratchett's witches: Granny Weatherwax, Nanny Ogg and Magrat Garlick. In another sense, it's the beginning of another unofficial trilogy (with *Maskerade* and *Carpe Jugulum*) about the mortality and power of Granny Weatherwax, with bonus Nanny Ogg at every turn and the growing pains of Agnes 'Perdita' Nitt.

Lords and Ladies is also, like so many of Pratchett's best books, a book about stories. Having already taken on Shakespeare and fairy tales, he addresses the roles of women in English folk songs and folklore. This is a story about cold iron and fairy glamour: of midsummer rituals and blood in the snow and dodgy innuendoes about Morris dancers and maypoles. It's a story about how practicality trumps romance every time, if you're lucky.

Most of all, while it has much to say about witches and wives and mothers, this is a story about queens.

I love the progression of Magrat in *Lords and Ladies*: she finds herself in the unexpected position of being engaged to a king, then awkwardly tiptoes around and through the question of what exactly a queen is supposed to do all day. There is a running commentary on the double standard, of how Verence can basically trot around 'with his arse out of his trousers', acting only slightly more regally than when he was a Fool. Meanwhile, the new queen has fashion requirements and antiquated traditions to juggle, not to mention the juxtaposition of high feminine status with officially sanctioned uselessness.

Scenes where Magrat and her hapless ladies maid try to figure out the ridiculous clothes, her position on embroidery, and so on, are both funny and poignant. But it turns quite tragic when Magrat believes that she has to leave her old life as a witch and healer behind, ridding herself of all her magical paraphernalia. She literally steps out of one identity and into another. Understandably, it messes with her head.

Pratchett is excellent at pointing out story tropes that are actually ridiculous if you try to fit ordinary people into them, and so *Lords and Ladies* comments not only on the traditional portrayal of queens in mythology, history and literature, but also on the shifting nature of women's identity when they marry.

Magrat's personal journey comes to a head with her discovery of Queen Ynci, a warrior queen archetype no one had told her about, and then again with her encounter with the royal beekeeper, who tells her the most fascinating details about the selection criteria for queen bees. When the chips are down and her royal husband is in danger, Magrat gets to emulate both Queen Ynci and the queens of beekind, becoming a true '*Slash! Stab!*' kickass heroine.

Alongside Magrat's personal journey is an ongoing narrative about how Granny Weatherwax and Nanny Ogg are trying to deal with the actual hazard (elves returning to the Discworld) while keeping Magrat in the dark, because of their perception of her as someone who believes ballads over real life. They assume she is going to believe elves are cute and romantic. And yes, that is her first reaction, and yes it does almost get her killed, but mostly because *the older witches never taught her otherwise*. While this is deeply frustrating, it's also a culmination of an ongoing character arc for the older witches over the last few books. They've never taken Magrat seriously, and Granny being wrong in this instance is vital to the plot. Because this is also the book in which Granny Weatherwax dies.

She doesn't die, of course—this is the book that made the 'I Aten't Dead' sign so legendary—but this is one of several Discworld novels in which the narrative leads Granny into her final battle—and, against all laws of narrative, she survives it. This particular final battle is resolved because of a different Granny in her head, one who married young instead of becoming a witch. Pratchett deals with what he likes to call 'the Trousers of Time' quite regularly, but this is the most compelling of his stories about alternate universes, and how a little knowledge of them can go a long way. It's important that Granny is wrong about Magrat, because it shows her vulnerability, which suggests that she might actually die.

For many, many books, we've been told that witches and wizards know when they're going to die—it's one of the essential facts of the Discworld. Here, Pratchett provides a major fake-out that, crucially, is also not a cheat. It's fascinating to see how he puts all the little pieces of this plot together, and how everyone's narrative circles back to the same repeated elements, all tied up into a beautiful bow.

Granny's impending (not) death is prefigured by the introduction of Diamanda, a teen Mean Girl who wants to be a witch but thinks it's all about black nail polish and looking glamorous. Because of this error in judgement, she lets loose sociopathic elves across the Ramtops.

Pratchett conveys a girl clique startlingly well, with the other girls dancing around Diamanda and desperate to copy her (much like bees around a queen, oh yes, THEME I SEE YOU) and we get our first introduction to Perdita/Agnes Nitt, who only appears in a few scenes, but shows herself to be the most pragmatic of the girls. In a book that's all about how Practicality Pwns Romance, it's clear we're supposed to like Agnes, and keep an eye on her in the future.

It's important that Granny is wrong about Magrat, but just as important that Magrat wins the day, because she has always been far more practical than the older witches gave her credit for. She's romantic, but she has learned to harness that appropriately and not let it get in her way.

The differences between the three witches are celebrated in this book, showing how each of their methods can be valid. In fact, the story is very much about relationships between women: pecking orders, cliques, love, rivalries, loyalty, generational divides, and how the memory of the young girl she was can very much affect the choices of an old woman.

My favourite part of *Lords and Ladies* is when Granny takes the unconscious Diamanda to Magrat:

> *'It's all very well a potion calling for Love-in-idleness, but which of the thirty-seven common plants called by that name in various parts of the continent was actually meant? The reason that Granny Weatherwax was a better witch than Magrat was that she knew that in witchcraft it didn't matter a damn which one it was, or even if it was a piece of grass. The reason that Magrat was a better doctor than Granny was that she thought it did.'*

EVEN THOUGH GRANNY has grossly underestimated Magrat's ability to be sensible in the face of elves, she trusts her medical abilities over her own, which is a hell of a thing for a woman her age to admit.

Towards the end of the book, Granny Weatherwax reveals that the inspirational Queen Ynci, who inspired Magrat to fight the elf queen, almost certainly never existed—and her spiky armour definitely is not authentic. But it doesn't matter whether she was real or not: the function of folklore to warn and educate as well as to entertain infuses this book, from the surreal *Midsummer Night's Dream* parody to the deadly morris dancers, the songs and traditions, and the vicious nature of the elves themselves.

There's also romance in the book—a romantic storyline for each of the witches. Our pragmatic, raunchy Nanny Ogg is courted by the younger and much shorter Casanunda the dwarf. He thinks he's worldly and experienced until he gets a load of what's going on in her brain. Then we get Ridcully the wizard being soppy and sentimental about what could have been between him and Esmeralda Weatherwax in another lifetime, almost getting them killed through his nostalgia. Meanwhile, Granny herself is hard-edged and practical, far more concerned with saving the world than getting all silly about that boy she once kissed. (Oddly, that reminds me somewhat of the relationship between Katniss and her boys in *The Hunger Games*.)

Then there's the newly betrothed Magrat and Verence. Their awkwardness and inability to have actual conversations with each other is balanced out by their slow journey towards being a married couple, which includes sending off for a book to teach them about sex since they are both inconveniently inexperienced in that department. This is a romance of two people being sensibly in love with each other, and I adore them. There should be more stories that show how some of the best romance can be practical, rather than all dramatic and eyes-across-a-crowded-room. Plus, when it comes down to it, Magrat saves her man. So there's a bit of epic folksong love story in there too.

Have I mentioned how much I love this book? It's funny,

clever, feminist and has so much to say about the power of story. The plot is perfect, down to the last detail. The relationship between beliefs and real magic is expressed powerfully, without suggesting that either of those are more important than the other. The adventure, the comedy and the romance all exist to serve the narrative of three extraordinary women.

> '*Elves are wonderful. They provoke wonder.*
>
> *Elves are marvellous. They cause marvels.*
>
> *Elves are fantastic. They create fantasies.*
>
> *Elves are glamorous. They project glamour.*
>
> *Elves are enchanting. They weave enchantment.*
>
> *Elves are terrific. They beget terror.*
>
> *Elves are bad.*'

3
WEREWOLF GLAMOUR & THE SEXING OF DWARVES

Guards! Guards! (1989)

Men at Arms (1993)

Feet of Clay (1996)

I ALWAYS LOVED the City Watch books of the Discworld series almost as much as those of the Lancre Witches. Vimes is a wonderful character, utterly broken down by life when we first meet him. He gradually pulls himself up by his bootstraps, but never loses his deep cynicism about the world.

The books are packed with other memorable characters: Nobby Nobbs who is a big mass of personality quirks mushed together into a smelly vest, cautious Sergeant Colon with a quip for every occasion, and the utterly adorable Carrot, a man so damned GOOD that bluebirds sing whenever he walks down the street. He's basically a Disney Princess. We also get some of the best appearances in the

Discworld of the Patrician, one of the most compelling evil overlords ever to exist in fiction, and some of the best stories centred around the city of Ankh-Morpork. All this and airtight plots, mostly based around police procedural or murder mystery structures. Pretty good stuff.

But what about the women?

Guards! Guards!, the first book featuring the City Watch, is light on when it comes to female characters. The most central woman in the whole story is Sybil Ramkin, dragon expert. She emerges as a fascinating, fully realised and complicated female character despite (it has to be said) the narrative's constant attempts to undermine her as a person and a woman. Each time Lady Sybil appears, she has to wade through a sea of fat jokes, posh lady jokes, lonely spinster jokes, and in some cases, all three at once. More than once, she is described vividly as something monstrous or other than human, including scenes from the point of view of the man she will marry in later books.

But Sybil proves to be awesome. She's not just aristocratic and dragon-obsessed and lonely and less than slender; she's also smart, brave, funny, generous, and a good person. I don't know how to feel about the final scene in which Vimes capitulates to her romantic expectations—it's gorgeously written, but I rankled at him admitting so reluctantly that he finds her attractive. She is pretty much described as a perfumed siege engine rather than a person. But I love her, I love him, and I do think their later relationship is one of the best things about these books (gosh I hope it still is, better brace myself for the visit of the suck fairy) so I will forgive the author for giving Sybil such a problematic debut.

The rest of the women in *Guards! Guards!* are invisible. We are told about Carrot's mother, his old girlfriend Minty, his new sort-of-girlfriend Reet, and his innocent friendship with the local brothel madam Mrs Palm and her 'many unmarried daughters', all through scenes in which they don't appear, via dialogue or his letters home. Likewise Mrs Colon is referenced but we don't meet her; she's basically an old school "Her Indoors" joke. The entire plot, about a man who uses another bunch of men to summon a dragon and overthrow the Patrician in favour of a fake king to rule them all, and the men who stop him, is a total cockforest. But this is a very early Discworld book, from the era where women were not getting roles other than sexy lamps, landladies and witches.

As I discussed in Chapter 1, later Discworld books are far more inclusive of female characters, and that holds true for the City Watch volumes too.

The most interesting gender issue of *Guards! Guards!* is dwarf sex. In the early days of the Discworld, there were several throwaway jokes about dwarves, and why people only ever see the 'males' of the species (ie: the gruff little men with large beards and pick-axes). Here, we learn that the female dwarves are all over the place, but are physically indistinguishable from male dwarves when clothed. While this is basically one long, multi-book bearded woman joke, Pratchett is to be credited in that he a) acknowledged how often in fantasy we see whole magical species which appear to be 100% male and b) eventually expanded on his joke about the tact required in dwarfish romances, exploring gender presentation, femininity and cultural norms of sex.

Sadly none of that development is in this book. Here dwarf courtship is mentioned only because Carrot's relationship with Minty is deemed inappropriate (he's human, though adopted by dwarves, and more than twice her size). This is dealt with in an incredibly patriarchal way—while their mothers are referenced, it's handled by the fathers. Pratchett has not yet worked out how a truly blind-to-gender society might function, and is falling back on default settings.

The gender of dwarves is mirrored in a final revelation about the mighty dragon tormenting the city, which is that she's a girl. In light of the other gender issues of this book, I found the handling of that revelation not just problematic but infuriating, not least because Pratchett serves up several fat jokes about the dragon INSTANTLY upon discovering her gender. Even worse, this revelation is treated as a reason to dismiss the valid danger of the dragon.

Gender should not actually make a difference to the fact that this is a monster we have seen wantonly destroying people and psychologically tormenting several other people. As soon as we learn that the dragon is female and that Errol the tiny swamp dragon isn't fighting her so much as courting her, however, we're supposed to go *awwww* and laugh about the variation in their sizes (as is mirrored with jokes about Carrot/Minty and Vimes/Sybil) and everything's okay. Sure, it's nice for Errol that he escaped with his mass-murdering girlfriend, but I remain troubled by that particular statement about gender.

Men at Arms, the second City Watch book, is notable for the introduction of Angua the werewolf. Sadly, Sybil's role has been diminished, and there's still no interesting exploration of dwarf sex.

The premise of *Men at Arms* (quite apart from the plot, which is about assassins, clowns, gentlemen and the Patrician, mostly male characters) is that the Ankh-Morpork City Watch are undergoing two major administrative changes: Vimes is stepping down to marry Sybil and become a Gentleman of Leisure, and the Patrician has brought in reforms which demand a greater representation of diversity among the guards. Thus the new recruits are A Troll, A Dwarf, and A Woman. Though of course Angua being female is a red herring—while Carrot and those readers not paying close attention assume she was hired for gender diversity, she was actually hired as a werewolf, representing of the Undead.

This inclusion of nonhumans in the City Watch will become a vital aspect of their identity in later books. The culture clashes are explored through several relationships, such as the growing tolerance/friendship of Lance-Constable Detritus (troll) with Lance-Constable Cuddy (dwarf) and particularly with the friendship and romance of Angua and Carrot.

On my recent reread, with this essay topic in mind (and because she is generally the first person most readers cite as an Awesome Discworld Woman), I found myself scrutinising the portrayal of Angua. She's handled unevenly in *Men at Arms,* which was a surprise to me as consistent characterisation is usually one of Pratchett's great strengths as an author, and I remembered this as being *her* book. But it feels ike the author hadn't decided what she was there for, and the male gaze is everywhere in the narrative. There are constant references to Angua 's knockout gorgeous good looks; the descriptions of her fall of loose blond hair are especially irritating. The character is practical—she'd tie her damn hair back for work. Likewise I wasn't happy about how often we are encouraged to think about Angua naked—

sure, that's a side effect of being a werewolf, but I was put off by the *snigger-snigger* tone of these scenes.

It's always uncomfortable to realise that a book is assuming its reader to be a heterosexual man.

Angua's point of view doesn't enter the book until quite late in the narrative—at first she's just part of the crowd, alternating between being the rookie who is sharper than everyone else (getting the dirty joke no one else does) to being the rookie who needs to have something quite simple explained. Her personality shifts for narrative convenience.

Once her point of view finally arrives, and we learn about how she functions as a werewolf and her bemused thoughts about Carrot, her character comes beautifully to life. She's smart and snarky, and her vulnerability about being a werewolf is countered by her resentment and sense of injustice. Angua really is a fantastic character; I was just surprised how long it took for us to get there.

Another problem I had with the narrative of *Men at Arms* is Carrot's blatant anti-undead sentiment. His character has been so untroubled by any other form of bigotry up until now, even those ingrained in him from being raised a dwarf. It seems odd that he is weirded out by Mrs Cake and her lot, but doesn't bat an eyelid about trolls being people too. So Angua isn't the only one whose character doesn't always make sense!

Their romance is handled effectively, and I like that it is about the meeting of two equals with radically different perspectives. The sex scene, which like all other Pratchett sex scenes is handled with so much discretion that you could blink and miss it, progresses both plot and character.

Despite my reservations about aspects of this storyline, I like that Carrot has to suck up and deal with his prejudices—not just about the undead, but about women. In the end, getting his head around Angua's strength and invulnerability is probably a bigger deal than her spending a few days a month as a canine.

Angua doesn't have to learn anything from this relationship because she's already great; sadly, this relegates her to supporting character rather than protagonist. Once she decides to sleep with Carrot, we don't get to see inside her head any more, and the story goes back to being about his reactions. It's a pragmatic romance than a soppy one, and doesn't assume a happy ever after. Still, Angua's friendship with Gaspode the Wonder Dog brings out far more honesty and personality in her than any of her scenes with Carrot...

It's disappointing to me that Sybil takes such a back seat in this novel, especially considering that her wedding to Vimes forms the climax of the story. We mostly only see Sybil as background to his crisis about how to fit into her world. We don't see them talk about, for instance, the fact that she has signed over her entire fortune to him (he finds this out from her bank manager), or that he has quit drinking to make her happy. It's Carrot, and not Sybil, who comes up with the idea of making Vimes a Knight and putting him back in charge of the expanded Watch, which is disappointing because she is left with so little agency. Mostly she worries about him, from afar.

By the time *Feet of Clay* comes along, the third City Watch book, Sybil has disappeared entirely. Like Mrs Colon, she has become an invisible wife, referred to when relevant, but staying out of the plot. The only consolation for this is the development of a far crunchier and more interesting relationship between Carrot and Angua, the long-awaited matter of DWARF SEX and the introduction of one of my favourite female friendships of the Discworld series.

Feet of Clay is an excellent novel—certainly better in plot and emotional depth than the previous City Watch books. It has a clever police procedural plot concerning a not-quite-assassination attempt on Lord Vetinari, and the community of golems in Ankh-Morpork. Along with the twists and turns of the mystery, the narrative contains a meta-commentary on police work in general. Everything *Guards! Guards!* and *Men at Arms* did well, *Feet of Clay* builds upon, almost perfectly.

The uneven characterisation of Angua in *Men at Arms* contrasts sharply with her portrayal here—we learn who she is and what kind of life she comes from, in telling details that don't detract from the main plot. Her central concern at the beginning of the novel is pretty much the same as it is by the end—she believes her relationship with Carrot has no future, and that she has to leave him soon, before it becomes too hard to break up. But she can't. It's never clear whether the reason she can't is because she loves him (as a woman), or because she is loyal to him (as a dog), and this is not resolved.

This would have been immensely frustrating, if that was the only thing Angua contributed to the novel. But along comes Cheery Littlebottom, whose friendship with Angua lights up the pages in between the golem angst and Vimes-related plottery.

We are introduced to Cheery as a male dwarf. Even the pronoun 'he' is used, which is not a cheat, because we have learned in previous books that all dwarves say 'he' as their default. But Cheery, as Angua with her werewolf nose spots instantly, is female. (It's not clear why Angua decides to make a thing of this for this dwarf in particular when there are other female dwarves in the Watch, nor why Cheery is terrified people might know, *when there are other female dwarves in the Watch*, but I don't care because it kickstarts my favourite ever sub-plot.)

Cheery is an alchemist hired by Vimes to be his forensics expert, a job they are making up as they go along. Cheery is deeply unhappy when we first meet her, because of her own perceived failures as a dwarf. She doesn't fit in with traditional dwarfish culture, and feels alienated from them because she is drawn to traditionally feminine pastimes. Female dwarves are equal to male dwarves in every possible way—but only because they look, act and appear exactly like male dwarves. Which, of course, is not equality. Angua draws a parallel to being a woman in the City Watch—you are allowed to be one of the boys, but only if you act just like them (or, rather, just enough like them to be part of the group, but not so much like them that they get intimidated).

With Angua's help and assistance, Cheery begins the process of coming out as a female dwarf. She experiments with gender presentation, which is largely played for laughs as the bemused male characters like Carrot and Vimes react to her jewellery, makeup and/or the wearing of a skirt. Still, there's a serious theme behind the humour. Cheery, or Cherie, or Cherry, as she sometimes chooses to be called, is deadly serious. There's a quite wonderful scene in which she faces off against a group of her fellow dwarves for the first time, bravely dealing with their disgust and disapproval, only for one to hang back afterwards and beg to try her lipstick. Because, of course, *she's not the only female dwarf in the Watch,*. By leading the way and taking the flak, she is able to give other dwarves the opportunity to present as female, if they want to.

She never contemplates shaving off her beard, of course. Because...it's her beard. She wants to present as female on her own terms, not just mimicking what human women do.

There's a running theme about the strength of women—another favourite scene of mine in this book shows a gang of angry, violent criminals in a tavern who grab Angua as a hostage. The tavern is full of her fellow Guards, who calmly watch, trusting her take care of herself. Even Carrot, who loves her, only reminds her not to kill anyone. It's a relief that Carrot has learned to overcome his natural chivalry because of Angua's strength and competence—and we see him begin that struggle again with his concern for Cheery in the field, where he would not have been so protective of a dwarf who presented as male.

Cheery's dwarfish aversion to werewolves, and Angua having to keep the secret from her despite knowing it is inevitable she will find out, makes sense in so many ways (it works much better than Carrot's prejudice in *Men at Arms*) and I liked that there is plenty of time devoted to the outcome of this deceit. This female friendship has to overcome serious obstacles and it is given the kind of narrative priority in the story that is usually devoted to a romance. Sromance, people! There should be more of it.

I love that the first forensic scientist of the Discworld is a woman—and along with the issues to do with her coming out story and gender performance/presentation, we witness her high level of competence at her job. Vimes quickly learns to rely on her for her alchemical skills and her flexibility. She's constantly coming up with new tests and techniques to match his crazy and inventive ideas about new police work. The running gag about Cheery/Cherie wearing earrings, or a skirt, or so on, could have detracted from this, but it never does. Vimes takes her experiments in his stride, and I get the impression that he would have done exactly the same if it were Sergeant Colon or Nobby who turned up to work in a frock.

The first three City Watch books feature three interesting, complex and thoroughly different female characters. Not bad for a series that is primarily about the agency of male characters— the push-pull of Vimes' relationship with the city and the Patrician who rules it; Carrot the uncrowned king, who is genuinely interested in everyone and wants to help them, but doesn't seem aware of the power of his own charisma; Nobby and Colon, Shakespearian clowns if ever there were any, and many more.

These are not books that were intended to be about women. But the women in them have so much potential and so much to say. I am heading now into less familiar territory, with several City Watch books I never read more than once (I loathed both *Jingo* and *The Fifth Elephant* the first time around, and don't remember a word of *Thud*) but I am hoping to find a book which gives me Sybil, Angua and Cheery all at once. Possibly it doesn't exist, but we'll see!

4
HIS HENPECKED VOICE

Jingo (1997)

The Fifth Elephant (1999)

BOTH *JINGO* and *The Fifth Elephant* missed their mark entirely with me when I read them on first release, so I had low expectations for my reread.

Jingo fared much better for me this time around. The prose is clever and tight, and there are crunchy themes about war, patriotism, etc. It's one of those Discworld books that transcends comic banter and set pieces to reveal a deeper philosophical meaning, plus as many Leonardo Da Vinci jokes as any sane person would ever want in one place.

However, the thing it doesn't have is much in the way of… you guessed it, women.

Sybil appears in a few scenes, in the role of nagging wife. I do like the bit where she chides Vimes for treating her as if she is nagging him and how unfair it is, but that's Sybil for you, grasping any attempt to be awesome, in the face of a book that is working against her. She is mostly here to react to how awkwardly/effectively Vimes is assimilating into the upper classes, and to wave a few warning flags that his workaholic lifestyle is unsustainable. This at least will be followed up in later books.

Cheery barely appears at all, with little follow up on her interesting debut back in *Feet of Clay*. Again, this will be addressed later.

Angua's role in *Jingo* is the greatest disappointment, as Pratchett does that thing where he introduces her POV early on and sets her character up with intriguing issues to deal with, and then largely forgets about her for the rest of the book. *This is not the only time he does that thing.* Worst of all, she is forced into the position of Captured Damsel, which is just insulting. I can see how the Watch and Carrot's attitude to Angua's invulnerability is the kind of complacency that begs to be challenged. However, when you start out with a subversively powerful female character, subverting her a second time to make her vulnerable and a captive is not actually all that revolutionary when she is, in fact, a blonde girl.

Angua rescues herself, but that doesn't make up for the fact that she is treated so badly for most of this story, and that we don't get enough of her point of view.

The most poignant and/or problematic treatment of women in *Jingo* is the sub-plot where Nobby Nobbs has to (well, 'has to' is perhaps too strong a phrase...) dress up as a woman as part of his spying activities for the Patrician. He is so stunned to see what life is like from this different perspective (especially how he is treated by the men around him, including those who know exactly who he is) that he turns into a radical suffragette and refuses to let go of his feminine identity.

I still haven't decided if this storyline is hilarious, offensive or a smart bit of characterisation. It's an oddity. It's also something Pratchett doesn't let go of, returning in later books to the cross-dressing (and occasionally feminist) tendencies of Corporal Nobbs.

Which brings us to *The Fifth Elephant*. I have no idea why I wasn't keen on this one the first time I read it, because while the story and writing isn't as tight as in *Jingo*, the book features major plotlines surrounding Angua, Sybil and Cheery, plus OTHER female characters, and that kind of awesomeness needs to be encouraged.

Sybil's role in this novel looks unpromising at first. The story revolves around the team going on a diplomatic junket to the mysterious Übervald, a country loosely based on Translyvania by way of Germany, France, Wales and judging by Stephen Briggs's voice performance (I'm still on the audiobook kick) basically anywhere with an accent. For the first part of the story, Sybil's role involves packing, unpacking, and settling in at the embassy. But while the idea of Vimes as a diplomat is a colossal joke, Sybil turns out to be really, really good at it. Her deep appreciation of dwarf opera is essential in a moment of diplomatic crisis, which is a wonderful turning point for her character, and her mighty heroics at the end are splendid.

Finally we get deeper appreciation of who Sybil is as a person. The very unpleasant Baroness von Übervald (AKA Angua's mum) sees her as a foolish, overly friendly person, and we later see her perceptions of Sybil's behaviour sharply deconstructed through Sybil's own point of view. It's important to get these scenes through Sybil's eyes, and indeed through those of the Baroness as well, because we were in danger otherwise of her character being largely presented to us through the eyes of Vimes.

The story of the Sybil-Vimes marriage gets some further development. Their obvious problem is that Vimes is married to his job first and to Sybil second, but we also witness some lovely scenes that show why their marriage works, and how it has improved life for both of them. My favourite is the scene told mostly through dialogue in which they, in bed at night, hear the various bumping noises happening in the embassy below them, and take turns guessing which of the appalling stuffed heads are being removed (at their request) based on sound alone.

There's also the running almost-joke about Sybil having something to tell Vimes, which she is finally able to do only at the end of the story: they are having a baby! This is telegraphed quite clearly and hardly likely to be a surprise to the reader, but that's not the point of this reveal. After a rather adorable exchange in which Vimes tries as diplomatically as possible (so not his strong point!) to ask how safe the pregnancy is considering her age, Sybil puts him down sharply by insisting that breeding is what her family were designed for, and he should stop asking silly questions. But now Vimes has to make a new choice about how to live his life, which we will see reflected in his later books. When they leave Übervald, rather than racing right back to his work at home, he offers Sybil a real holiday by suggesting they travel back by the slower, touristy route (as Nanny Ogg would put it, they went the long way and saw the elephant). Vimes as a father is going to try more strenuously to achieve a work-life balance than he did in his early days of marriage, and this is the first sign that he is willing to make that change.

I am glad for all the Sybil awesomeness in *The Fifth Elephant* because I wasn't happy with how Angua's storyline was handled. This is the book that takes us to Angua's home, and shows us her family. I find it really bizarre, then, that so much of her story is told without her own involvement. She disappears from Ankh-Morpork, leaving the focus of the story on Carrot and Gaspode's quest to find her. When she and Carrot finally get to talk about why she left, how this ties in with her family history, and their relationship, the whole scene is told from the point of view of Gaspode the freaking Wonder Dog.

Now, I'm a big fan of Gaspode. And this ties into Pratchett's traditional method of using the omniscient point of view—he has the choice of his characters, so usually chooses the one whose take on the scene is most likely to be funny. Fair enough. But it's only since I started these essays looking specifically at the portrayal of female characters in the Discworld that I realise the downside of his technique. Pratchett sometimes uses a character's point of view only a few times, and doesn't always follow up on them—Angua is a constant casualty of this.

It could be argued that this works just fine. There is a theme running through the book that Angua is not talked about amongst her family, as Vimes notices when he tries to mention her to her mother. Angua is also a private person. There is no denying that, by the end of the novel, there is a great deal of resolution about her problems with Carrot (I am giving her the benefit of the doubt and suggesting that her complaints about him being too nice and tolerant are masks for her real concerns about the unsustainable nature of their relationship, otherwise she does come off as pretty damn unreasonable in their fight) and her feelings about her family.

But...yeah. There are gaps in the story that could only be filled by a little more Angua. Considering that one of the main bad guys is her brother and fellow werewolf, and that trying to kill him so that he stays dead is a main thrust of the final act of the story, it's disappointing that we get to see so little of that story through her eyes. This was not the satisfying Angua book I wanted it to be, and I think that *Feet of Clay* remains a better showcase for her character.

Thank goodness for Cheery! Our favourite feminine dwarf has some wonderful scenes, and while she doesn't quite have a full storyline of her own, her subplot is dealt with so cleverly and with such thoughtfulness that it brings me joy. She also steals the scene at the end when the dwarf politics storyline turns out to be far more relevant to Cheery's gender choices than anyone suspected.

Basically, if you found the 'coming out as a female dwarf' plot strand in *Feet of Clay* interesting, then *The Fifth Elephant* has it in spades, if you hang in there until the end. We experience Cheery's discomfort and rebellious bravery in returning to her homeland of Übervald as an openly female dwarf. The Ankh-Morpork dwarf community, which has fast adapted to the trend of femininity despite some resistance, is far more liberal than those dwarves back home. Dwarf culture is something Pratchett has put a lot more thought into since *Guards! Guards!*, and I love the idea that their greatest romantic opera is between two

DWARVES, making it culturally important not to question which of the two dwarves was female.

Which leads to the double whammy reveal at the end of the story. The dwarf who perpetuated a key crime is a woman, partly motivated by frustration at how the changing times has allowed other dwarves to reveal and revel in their own femininity. Then we discover that the quietly liberal king they have managed to keep on the throne is, say it with me, ALSO A WOMAN.

Pratchett loves a juicy gender reveal, challenging default assumptions. Later (and I will get there eventually) he structures an entire novel around that reveal, over and over again. This trope allows him to say (and not say) a great deal about gender politics, and I find that fascinating because for the most part these kind of gender-bending tricks are found in the literature of hardcore feminist writers.

It started out as a joke, but as with many Pratchett jokes, it's a soft centre wrapped around a sharpened axe.

I want to squee more about Cheery, but I'm running out of space. Suffice to say: I love that she fills the role of Sybil's lady's maid with enthusiasm; I love the scene at the end where she decides to dress 'as a dwarf' (ie: present as male) in front of the king because while she knows she will have the support of her friends and allies if she wears a dress, she has moved past feeling the need to do so for every single occasion; and I LOVE the fact that her first response to the reveal about Dee (the villain dwarf) is to comfort her, one girl to another.

Most of all I love that, as Cheery is only a little embarrassed about, that she used that comforting gesture to give Dee a chance to hand over really important information. She's a dwarf, and a woman, but she's also a damn good copper, and that comes before all the other things.

Cheery Littlebottom may well be my favourite Discworld character now. I so didn't see that coming.

Other female-character-highlights of *The Fifth Elephant* include the glamorous vampire-on-the-wagon Lady Margalotta, and Angua's bitchy Baroness mother. Nice to have some antagonist characters in these books who are female from the start, rather than only being revealed in the last five pages.

5
A WONDERFUL PERSONALITY AND GOOD HAIR

Maskerade (1995)

Carpe Jugulum (1998)

MASKERADE MAKES me cranky that Magrat's marriage has pushed her out of the narrative of the Lancre witches, but it's hard not to be delighted about the arrival of Agnes 'Perdita' Nitt. She's a fantastic character, one of Pratchett's most interesting and nuanced portrayals of a younger female protagonist.

Agnes is fat. And while Pratchett's comic touch is very much in evidence, he brings such empathy to his depiction of Agnes that, even when fat jokes are flying around, she herself is never treated like a joke. This is an incredibly rare thing in fantasy fiction, where fat women are rarely seen (unless they are villains, motherly matrons or jolly service industry professionals) and young fat women don't exist at all.

There are so many things to like about the portrayal of Agnes in this book. For a start, we don't get the clichéd emphasis on how she eats, or an ingrained narrative assumption that she is the size she is purely through overeating or laziness. I also appreciate that while the reader is often confronted with the quite awful social ramifications of being a fat girl, it's never entirely clear-cut how much the various perceptions surrounding Agnes reflect reality.

Nanny Ogg, for example, a larger lady herself, muses on how Agnes is a better bet for joining the witches because she's less likely to lose her maiden status than so many other village girls... but almost in the same breath acknowledges that fatness is no particular barrier to finding a husband in the Ramtops, especially if that corresponds with a talent for cooking. Nanny's own figure has never put men off—even at her advanced age, she's batting men away with her broomstick.

Likewise, while the plot revolves partly around Agnes being less 'stage-worthy' than the tone-deaf but thin and beautiful Christine, and thus having to provide her with a fake singing voice from behind the curtain, we hear regularly about the famous (fat) opera singer Gigli, and how she is desired for her luscious appearance as well as her beautiful voice.

The undercurrent of the story is that it's not Agnes' weight getting in the way of her happiness—it's Agnes. She certainly is discriminated against because of her weight, and experiences some hurtful and embarrassing moments throughout the story, her ACTUAL problem is the wonderful personality that everyone keeps going on about ('a wonderful personality and good hair' being a euphemism for 'not thin enough, not pretty enough').

Agnes doesn't leave the Ramtop Mountains and come to the big city to audition as an opera singer because she is fat, or can't get a boyfriend, and it becomes evident pretty quickly that it's not entirely because she dreams of musical stardom, either. Opera isn't her first choice, it's just something to do. She is desperate to find herself an independent future that has nothing to do with the witches Granny Weatherwax and Nanny Ogg, who are looking for a third member of their coven—but even before the two of them strike out to follow her to the big city, she can't escape the witches because she is already one of them.

At every turn, it's not Agnes' weight that is the problem, but her brain. She can't turn off the cynical voice that always says the wrong thing; the sharp inner bitchiness that sees all the daftness in the world for what it is. This, clearly, is what made it less likely she would find a boy to lose her "maiden" status too, and not her full figure.

The joke is repeated (a touch too often) that inside every fat girl is a thin girl trying to get out— the one inside Agnes is called Perdita, the pseudonym she chooses for the theatre. Perdita is her imaginary ideal self.

Agnes is a very intelligent girl who grew up in a village where getting married was the main concern of her peers, and she has escaped to a world where music and looking pretty are the only concern, because the fate of an intelligent girl in her village (becoming a witch) feels dreadful to her. Inventing 'Perdita' and joining the opera allows her to feel she has some control over her fate and her identity.

Gradually, as the shine of opera starts to wear off and Agnes discovers that they're all basically crazy and making her crazy too, serving the capricious god that is 'opera' starts to feel as onerous as serving Nanny and Granny as their third witch. Right on cue, in the elder witches march to demonstrate to Agnes that being a witch isn't as terrible a life as it looks from the outside. Being a witch means being the smart person in the village who is allowed to say the wrong thing any time they like, and has the ability to help people even if they don't think they want to be helped.

Being a witch means being the person who says 'WHY must the show go on?' when everyone else is running around like headless chickens and enjoying the melodrama. In short, everything Agnes wanted from her mythical 'Perdita' is waiting for her in the job description of 'witch'. She just has to stop sabotaging herself.

There's a lot of pantomime and humour in the portrayal of the two elder witches, but it's nice to get some insight into the characters of Granny Weatherwax and Nanny Ogg as a unit, as friends, and also as women who probably shouldn't spend too much time alone together. I love to watch the different ways they approach the mystery: Granny goes directly for the insides of people's heads, while Nanny watches their body language and behaviour.

The sympathy they feel for Mrs Plinge, the woman who knows pretty much everything that's going on in the theatre and suffers through her own personal tragedy every day, comes across clearly, and that's important because it tells us that Agnes is at least partly wrong about them.

I'm uncomfortable with the characterisation of thin girls in this book—though I will admit to having a soft spot for the line about how the ballerinas are crazed with hunger. It would be nice to have a book that deals positively with fat female characters without judging and deriding thin women.

Christine's thinness gives her unfair advantage over Agnes, though she is not an unsympathetic character. Her presence shows us how thin privilege works: Agnes is overlooked and misses out on opportunities, while opportunities are thrown in Christine's way. Christine takes her 'luck' for granted without questioning its source, and is often thoughtless in how she accepts the rewards for her beauty, but is never deliberately cruel. Those who can see how much of her 'luck' is due to her beauty tend to resent and despise her for it, or want to possess her because of how she looks.

Christine's innocence and generosity is what salvages the character from being a Pretty Girl cliché—she is a good friend to Agnes, despite the competitive situation they are in (and Agnes, thanks to the urging of Perdita, is less than a good friend to her). Agnes might be the one who is blessed with 'a good personality' but of the two, Christine is the only one who behaves like a nice person. Of course, Christine can afford to be nice, because everything she ever wants falls into her lap...see? NUANCE. I am impressed once again to see a story this complex about the interactions of women told by a male author.

In the end, while we know that Agnes has decided to submit to the witches and join them, she is not prepared to go home on their terms. The final scene of her drenched in mud and rain while they speed home in the comfy coach shows her stubbornness and tenacity, as well as her general tendency to cut off her nose to spite her face. She is going to be a very different kind of third witch than Magrat.

And, speaking of Magrat...

It's funny how motherhood completely changes your perspectives on what's relevant, and important. I remembered that *Lords and Ladies* was the last time Magrat got to shine, and that once she got married, she disappeared out of the narrative of the Lancre witches. I also remembered that *Carpe Jugulum* was mostly dull, with a few good Granny Weatherwax bits, and not much else of interest.

How wrong I was!

Carpe Jugulum is one of those Discworld books (like *Hogfather*) where the mystery doesn't work as a murder mystery should; it's far more powerful and effective in the reread when you know what's going on. Granny Weatherwax is under attack from some very smooth vampires who are determined to take control of Lancre from under her nose. She responds by disappearing, apparently surrendering her power, leaving the three remaining witches in the kingdom to come together and save the day.

The sneaky twist being that when the vampires bite Granny and leave her for dead, she manages to infect them instead of vice versa, so they start saying things like 'I can't be having with this' and craving tea. She turns a whole pack of slavering ageless vampires into cranky old ladies.

This is a brilliant narrative choice. Our culture now has many, many stories of a woman getting the better of a pack of vampires, of which Buffy the Vampire Slayer is the most iconic example. Any attempt to subvert that popular trope would result in the same horrid double subversion that turned Sergeant Angua into a damsel in *Jingo*.

Here, Pratchett subverts the 'female victim gets the better of the vampires' trope by employing a completely passive method—Granny literally lies down and lets them drink her blood—and allows the results to be devastating. It's one of the best examples I can think of how the 'strong women characters' trope has rendered so many types of female strength invisible—any female hero who acts other than violent and aggressive (while also being sexy) is often derided by critics as a weak, passive or sexist character, while those who act in traditionally masculine/active ways are treated as the only female heroes worth celebrating. This is especially the case, sadly, in SF and fantasy media.

I discovered to my surprise that this is now my favourite Granny Weatherwax book, despite the lack of her in a fair chunk of the story. Whenever she does appear, she is mesmerising. Her not-quite-friendship-let's-say-alliance with the hapless priest Oats is compelling to watch, especially because he is the only person not in awe of her reputation—he perceives her as an old lady who needs help (which for once is true), and has to figure out ways to circumvent her ego in order to help her, because *she* can't accept that she is vulnerable.

Oats is probably the most interesting male character ever to interact with the witches, not least because each of them react very differently to him: with Granny he is the outsider who sees her more clearly than anyone else; with Nanny there is ongoing religious disagreement because of his Church's history of burning witches; and with Agnes there is a sort-of-maybe romantic tension, which remains largely unaddressed because they are equally incapable of allowing their interest to rise above subconscious level. (Plus she spends most of the book batting a hot vampire away with a broomstick.)

But there are four witches in this story, not three. Magrat begins the story as the ex-witch, concentrating on her new baby's christening and other queen things. But as the vampires take over the kingdom and her husband (yet again!) falls victim to magical predators (let me tell you how much I love the constant damselling of Verence in these books) Magrat has to put on her big witch knickers, strap her baby to her back and save the day.

As someone who has been doing the mother-of-small-children thing in recent years, I've become fascinated with how rare it is to see mums with babies on the front line in magical stories, and how they deal with it when it happens. (I really do have to get around to that article I've been meaning to write on Gwen Cooper and working motherhood in *Torchwood: Miracle Day*.)

The problem with incorporating babies into magical adventure stories is that there is little excuse, most of the time, for taking the baby into danger. Unless of course, there is nowhere safe to leave the baby, which is the situation here! Young Esme is much safer strapped to her mother's back, with Nanny Ogg at her side, than being babysat by anyone else in a kingdom full of vampires. Indeed, getting the baby to safety becomes a driving part of the plot, leading them into worse danger.

There's an ongoing thread about how Magrat isn't a virgin any more, and thus understands a lot more of Nanny Ogg's dirty jokes than she used to. Given how much focus the

Lancre Witches novels place upon the roles of maiden, mother and crone, it's nice to see some exploration as to how the transition into mother or crone can be, well, perspective changing!

Then there's Agnes. In *Maskerade*, Perdita is presented as Agnes' inner voice, the one who says the bitchy and intelligent things she normally tries to damp down. By *Carpe Jugulum*, it's clear that Perdita has become a powerful character in her own right, as much as a cross for Agnes to bear as the overwhelming personalities of Granny Weatherwax and Nanny Ogg.

Perdita also has a role to play in the plot, as the only one immune to the mesmerism of the vampires. Her resistance alerts Agnes to what is going on, and allows her to help the other witches resist. I am glad to see that now she is a witch, Agnes has taken back her inner snark as part of her own personality, leaving the inner Perdita with the more romantic and impractical views on life. Their interactions are quite fascinating, and I am sad that Pratchett leaves the characters here—he continues using Granny Weatherwax in the Tiffany Aching books, and even Nanny and Magrat get a tiny epilogue in those books, but this is the last time we see Agnes.

Considering the thematic importance of Agnes' weight in *Maskerade*, it's refreshing that it's not remotely relevant to *Carpe Jugulum*. The only time her fatness even referred to is when the bitchy female vampire Lacrimosa uses it to insult her—and that tells us a lot more about Lacky than Agnes. Meanwhile, Lacky's brother Vlad spends most of the book trying to seduce Agnes, and there are implications of a quieter and less showy potential romance between she and

Oats. Romantically desirable fat women in fantasy fiction for the win!

There's so much to like about *Carpe Jugulum*, which challenges the mythological traditions of vampires, and argues that a world in which the vampires are organised, methodical and POLITE about taking the blood of their victims is far more horrific than one where they are openly monstrous.

One of my favourite feminist moments of the Discworld occurs in this book—well, two of them. The first is Granny Weatherwax taking out a horde of vampires by lying down and letting them bite her; the second is the big finale, where Vlad is trying to convince Agnes to let him escape, because the possibility of romance always trumps personal safety, right?

> *Vlad looked imploringly at Agnes, and reached out to her.*
>
> *'You wouldn't let them kill me, would you? You wouldn't let them do this to me? We could have... we might... you **wouldn't**, would you?'*
>
> *The crowd hesitated. This sounded like an important plea. A hundred pairs of eyes stared at Agnes.*
>
> *She took his hand. **I suppose we could work on him,** said Perdita. But Agnes thought about Escrow, and the queues, and the children playing while they waited, and how evil might come animal sharp in the night, or greyly by day on a list...*
>
> *'Vlad,' she said gently, looking deep into his eyes. 'I'd even hold their coats.'*

6

THE SEAMSTRESS REDEMPTION

Night Watch (2002)

DERIDERS of the Bechdel Test tend to gravitate immediately towards what I like to call the *Shawshank Redemption* Clause. They cite as many works as possible that are completely awesome, and have no ladies in them, as evidence that the test is stupid.

Me, I see that as evidence that their faces are stupid. Also that they have missed the point of the Bechdel Test.

No one would deny that it's possible to create a masterpiece that has no women in it. However...there are few true masterpieces in the world, and there are almost no stories in the world that are so VERY amazingly perfect that they couldn't be improved by having more than one interesting female character.

I had this in my head upon revisiting *Night Watch*, because I remembered very clearly that a) this is primarily a story about men and b) this is one of my favourite Discworld novels of all time. I say this as someone who is meh about *Small Gods* and *Reaper Man*, two of the most celebrated of the Discworld novels, precisely because the overwhelming focus on male characters and male gaze left those books, in my opinion, lacking something.

Mostly, I was scared that my focus on female characters would spoil this book. It's not like it would be the first thing that my developing feminist perspective has utterly ruined for me.

But it turned out okay. Because (spoilers, sweetie!) *Night Watch* is still awesome. It's mostly a male narrative, AND it's awesome.

(As it happens, it passes the Bechdel Test. Just.)

This was the book, way back when, that got me excited about the Discworld and Pratchett's writing after a long dry spell of not loving his books any more. *Night Watch* is not a book to give to Discworld newbies. It does, however, contain some of Pratchett's most understated and subtle prose, it is the quintessential Vimes book, it's a time travel narrative that makes actual sense, and it reveals a secret history that links a whole bunch of Ankh-Morpork personalities in all manner of revealing ways.

Mostly the men.

I think that by this stage in his career, even in a novel all about war and police and serial killers and fatherhood and mentorship and men men men, Pratchett had become incapable of reaching for the easy sexist defaults that adorned his early books. Here, he gives us a whole subplot based around the Seamstresses (a socially accepted metaphor for prostitutes) who have been a background joke in every Ankh-Morpork book to date (the City Watch books in particular), and he humanises them.

We meet Rosie, the young woman who will eventually grow up to be Mrs Palm, the most notorious madam in the city and Carrot's unseen landlady back in *Guards! Guards!* Rosie is a fabulous character—confident, intelligent and cynical— and despite the book's nudge-nudge-wink-wink attitude to her profession, she is never portrayed in a degrading or sexualised way. This does have a lot to do with so many scenes being shown through the point of view of Vimes, who is so utterly married that everyone can see it from ten blocks away, but I respect the fact that there is no attempt to make their interactions flirty, or anything other than a wary alliance and almost-friendship.

Then there are the Agony Aunts, a vicious pair of head cases who work as heavies and protectors for the Seamstresses, under the employ of a mysterious lady known mostly as Madam. I loved these two, a great example of the kind of freaky throwaway background characters that Pratchett does so well. I especially liked that they didn't have to be female. He could have done anything to illustrate 'infamous comedy enforcers' but he went with terrifying old ladies, like the Kray brothers but with scones and knitting.

Another strong if minor female character is Sandra, who provides payoff for a decade of cheap jokes about "seamstresses". She's the real seamstress who actually does darning and mending, a rarity in the city because the others are sick of being mistaken for sex workers and have gone off to live in other cities. The scene in which she and Rosie discuss a sexual reference Sandra didn't understand (mirroring a similar scene between Vimes and his younger self) is the one that helps the book to technically pass the Bechdel Test. And of course there's more to Sandra than meets the eye—as Vimes discovers when he starts wondering why her laundry basket is so heavy.

Madam is a fascinating character, and her relationship to the young assassin Vetinari (her nephew) tells us a lot about his past and the formation of his character. The plot about the conspiracy to put a new Patrician on the throne is heavy with irony, and serves to demonstrate to Vimes as well as the reader why the present Vetinari's rule is so important. I liked that the Seamstresses are motivated by wanting to set up their own Guild (something we know to exists back in the future), and that the book shows off their political deviousness.

Cheery, like Angua, doesn't have much of a role in this book, because they are both too young and new to the Watch to be a part of the time period that Vimes visits. However, there is an adorable scene with Cheery at the very beginning of the book, which made me crazy happy.

The whole Watch is on the lookout for a dangerous man, and when he is located, Vimes is horrified to discover that Cheery is the officer on the spot. Not because she's female (that thought doesn't enter his head) but because she's the forensics officer, not 'street' and will do things by the book, which this particular criminal will use against her. When Vimes gets there, however, he finds that Cheery has made a succession of very smart and practical decisions as to the distribution of officers and resources. This time, when Vimes thinks the word 'forensic' to himself, it's with a small nod of respect.

So yes, Cheery is only in the novel for five minutes, but she kicks competent arse!

Finally, there is Doctor Lawn, who is male, but whose involvement in the story is all about women's issues. Apart from him being a cynical, entertaining character in his own right (an excellent foil for Vimes), the good doctor specialises in gynaecological services, including (as conveyed in a very understated conversation) contraception and abortion. Considering how often prostitutes are glamorised and set up as sex object window dressing in bog-standard fantasy fiction (the kind that Pratchett's work has reacted against from the beginning) I thought it important to note that these issues are addressed as a necessary side effect of looking closely at the role of prostitution in society. I also appreciated that this necessity was kept separate from any moral judgement on the part of the characters or the author.

However, I am uncomfortable with the scene at the end where Vimes calls one last time upon his friendship with Doctor Lawn. Childbirth can be dangerous, and it is absolutely one of the highest-stakes moments in many people's lives, but the portrayal of it in fantasy and science fiction (not to mention pop culture generally) is hugely problematic. One of the over-used tropes is the childbirth scene becoming about the man and what he can do to save the day, rather than being about the woman doing all the work.

I can forgive Sybil's labour and birth being turned into a panicky mercy dash scene that's all about Vimes—after all, he is the protagonist of this book, which is *his* story about impending fatherhood with extra metaphors coming into play after he becomes the man who once taught his younger self how to be a good policeman. And I am pleased that the birth of young Sam serves as an occasion to bring closure to Vimes' friendship with Doctor Lawn, just as the scene with the Patrician cleverly provides closure to all the other important bits of the time travel aspect of the novel (though I would have LOVED to see Vimes talking to an adult Mrs Palm, as Rosie is the only character he spends a lot of time with in the past who doesn't get closure at the end of the book).

But the thing that breaks *Night Watch* a tiny bit for me, the thing I can't entirely forgive, is the way that Sybil's (unseen) previously competent and practical midwife proves to be suddenly lacking, and it is the doctor who is brought in to save the day. I especially found myself grinding my teeth when Doctor Lawn lectures everyone about the revolutionary practice of boiling everything and promoting good hygiene. In the history of midwifery, THIS IS NOT WHAT HAPPENED. In fact, when the male doctors elbowed the mostly-female midwifes away from involvement in childbirth during the Victorian era, maternal death skyrocketed because of the increase of infections, thanks to doctors not bothering to wash their hands before or after vaginal examinations.

Sure, this is one story, and it works. The narrative is completely cohesive, and the conclusion of *Night Watch* wouldn't be as satisfying without this scene. Not a word is wasted. It's great writing. But it bugs me, because we end up with yet another narrative in which men know better than women about the female body. I expect better than this from Pratchett when it comes to remembering the sticky bits of human social history. I suspect, in fact, that this is another case of the Double Subversion problem (as seen with Sergeant Angua in *Jingo*) where the character of the doctor is deliberately set up to be a contrast to Pratchett's previously conveyed attitudes towards medicine, midwifery, women and witchcraft (say, in the Witches books) and the double subversion means that the character ends up reinforcing a tired and dangerous stereotype.

I feel like I haven't touched on many of the most important aspects of this story, and why it works so wonderfully well. There's a reason for that. My remit for these posts is to look at the portrayal of women in the Discworld books, and while I find the portrayal of women in *Night Watch* interesting, what makes it such a spectacular Discworld novel has nothing to do with the women at all. *Night Watch* has more women and female issues in it than I remembered, and for the most part (with that one glaring, flawtastic exception) those women and issues are handled respectfully. It's not quite one of those masterpieces that couldn't be improved with a greater involvement of female characters, but it is a very, very good book. And I still love it. Hooray!

7

HAS SCYTHE, WILL TEACH SCHOOL.

Soul Music (1994)

Hogfather (1996)

Thief of Time (2001)

REREADING all three of the Susan Sto Helit (or Susan Death) books was something I had been greatly looking forward to. I've always enjoyed Susan as a character even when I don't especially love the books she featured in—*Soul Music*, for instance, is not a favourite of mine, though the animated version of it is dear to my heart (funnily enough it DOES work better as a musical with a genuine soundtrack), *Hogfather* is one I've often found bewildering with moments of occasional joy, and before this reread I didn't remember anything about *Thief of Time*.

This time around, I enjoyed all three, but thanks to the theme of these essays, I couldn't help noticing that, well.

Considering what a popular and memorable character

Susan is, it's interesting how small a space she takes up in each of 'her' books.

Discworld novels are always ensemble productions; this is part of their charm. But it was a shock to discover that while Susan grows up and develops into an awesome adult from book to book, the books are never actually about her—she's not a protagonist, but fills the role of mentor/helper.

In each book, Susan starts out with a vivid and interesting introduction, then wanders in and out of the rest of the book being cross at people, exchanging banter with the minor supporting cast and not getting in the way of the plot; finally at the end she is generally unleashed as part of an epic showdown which is keyed to her talents, allows for character development, and shows how awesome she is.

I don't want to fall into the trap of reviewing books negatively for not meeting my own (possibly unrealistic) expectations, but this is so interesting to me in the light of how iconic Susan has become. She is, for instance, the young female character most often cited to me as an example of 'strong women in the Discworld'.

We first meet Susan in *Soul Music*, where she is a schoolgirl with mysterious abilities and a sharp tongue. She's immediately fantastic on the page—sarcastic and intelligent but guarded, all her secret hurts piled up inside where no one, even the reader, can get access to them.

Soul Music is a sequel to *Mort*, one of the most narratively satisfying and well plotted of the early Discworld novels; it's generally regarded as the one where the series 'got good'. *Mort* is about Death's apprentice, who fails at the job, but succeeds awkwardly in hooking up with Death's adopted daughter Ysabell (this potential marriage is the reason he is hired in the first place). A key plot point revolves around Mort's inability to accept the needs of the Duty, and how he wrongly saves the life of an assassinated princess, throwing reality into a tailspin because of a pretty face. At the end of his book, he dies and Death turns the hourglass over to give him more time, but mathematics are a bitch, and that means he's probably only going to get as much time again as he has already had...

Susan's story in *Soul Music* mirrors the story of Mort, her father. Shortly after both her parents are killed in a carriage accident, she is left to pick up the pieces when her grief-stricken Grandfather (Death) abandons the Duty in order to 'forget'. Susan acquires the scythe, the rat and her Grandfather's job...and starts to remember all those odd family visits from when she was very young.

Susan's storyline, and Death's storyline, are both subplots. The main plot of *Soul Music* is about how a young musician, Buddy, is possessed by an ancient evil inside a guitar and invents Music With Rocks In with a little help from his band. This is one of several Discworld novels featuring a magical pop culture invasion. It looks like Susan, who is rather taken with Buddy, is going to save him from assassins just as her father did for Princess Keli—but she doesn't. The music saves him instead, and warps reality. Rather than being the cause of the disaster, Susan is the one who cleans up the mess.

Susan stays mostly in the background of her debut novel, only occasionally crossing paths with the Band (to be mistaken as a groupie) until the final act.

Soul Music passes the Bechdel Test, as there is a scene early on where Susan talks with her headmistress, another with her school friends, and a very cute one with a Valkyrie who reminds her of a gym mistress, but the majority of her scenes involves her interacting with men or male characters: Albert, the rat and the raven; the Band; Ridcully and the wizards, Death.

The climax of the story is very much about Susan and Death coming to an accord, and sharing/understanding their mutual loss—as well as resolving the elephant in the room, which is that Death allowed his own family to die. Buddy and the Band literally fade out as the story is revealed to have been about Susan and Death and their issues all along. However, I'm not convinced that the two plots had enough to tie them together, despite some clever uses of thematic resonance to pretend they are part of the same story.

Revealing at the end of a book that someone is actually the protagonist is not quite as effective as letting her be the protagonist all the way through.

Susan and Buddy are worth mentioning because of their blink-and-you'll-miss-it romance, which is a pattern repeated across the Susan stories—when attracted to young men, she will typically show no outward sign of this attraction whatsoever, and so it tends not to go anywhere. In this case, the story ends on a note that suggests that the two of them might have a future in which they at least know each other (a low bar for a successful relationship, even in the Discworld) but we never hear of him again.

In *Hogfather*, the Discworld is under yet another magical threat, mostly involving male characters. Death removes himself from the equation again, leaving Susan to pick up the scythe and take over. It's basically *Soul Music* with Hogswatchnight (the Discworld Christmas) and the Tooth Fairies, instead of Music With Rocks In. The wizards even leap about in yet another a slapstick subplot.

I've never loved *Hogfather*—it belongs to an era of Discworld novels that I did not appreciate upon first read, and it's one of those Pratchett novels like *Carpe Jugulum* that actually makes no sense until you're reading it for the second or third time. I know it's a beloved favourite for many, but for me everything cool about it (like the conflagration of mythologies and folklore) is done far better in other Discworld novels.

Having said that, *Hogfather* has some excellent bits, and Susan is magnificent even if once again she is relegated to the role of helper/mentor/tidy-upper-of-disasters and isn't allowed to play with the plot-relevant main characters for more than short bursts.

What most irritates me about *Hogfather* is not that Susan isn't the protagonist, it's that there is no protagonist at all— or if there is, then it is the crazed assassin Teatime, who is a very unpleasant character to follow around. For this reason I think I prefer the TV movie to the book, because of not being in anyone's head, plus the bonus of Michelle Dockery's fabulous eyebrows. I always mean to make *Hogfather* the book a Christmas reading tradition as I know many Pratchett fans do, but never make myself do it. The movie, however, I can definitely see myself making part of an annual ritual.

Ahem. But let's get back to talking about the book. The Susan we meet in *Hogfather* has moved beyond her schooldays to become a governess, and the scenes in which she does this actively are the best in the book. It makes me wonder how governesses who don't have eldritch powers possibly cope with the requirements of the job, particularly when it comes to dealing with monsters under the bed.

(Victorian Clara in the *Doctor Who* story "The Snowmen" has to be at least partly based on Susan Death, whom she resembles far more than Mary Poppins.)

Susan's steely practicality is shown to great effect when she and little Twyla give one particular monster a good seeing to with the poker, while the ignorant parents and their upper crust friends think the whole thing is an amusing bit of child psychology. It's worth noting that young Twyla and Tooth Fairy Violet are the only female characters Susan interacts with, and neither have more than a couple of scenes in the book.

There's a fair bit of psychology (or in Discworld terms, Headology) going on in this book. Susan's childhood and her lack of romanticism turn out to be useful for this particular adventure, which revolves around the childhood belief in the Hogfather. The skills she has picked up from wiping little noses and pinning up brightly coloured paintings (not to mention telling improbable stories to wide-eyed four-year-olds) turn out to be vital survival skills, a twist I appreciate as a mother myself.

Once again, Susan appears in fewer scenes than I expected, and while she is the one who fights Teatime with her ruthless governessing skills, more than once, it still doesn't feel like she is being treated like a hero or a protagonist by the narrative. Her interactions with Bilious, the Oh God of Hangovers, follow the pattern of Susan's super-subtle romances (to be fair this one is so subtle I'm not even sure it's supposed to be read that way) and he falls happily in love with someone else over the course of the story. Susan's reaction is a quiet and understated deflation as if she hadn't even decided if she liked him yet, and is determined to be nothing more than mildly wistful about his sudden attachment to the rather soppy Tooth Fairy Violet.

More and more, Susan is outside the human race, looking in.

While the book as a whole is quite uneven, I do love the ending of *Hogfather*, where Susan beats Teatime in the traditional scythe-wielding way in the Tooth Fairy's castle, and then has to save the day for a second time by rescuing the mythic version of the Hogfather in form of a frightened wild boar, and then after all that, it's third time lucky when the threat turns domestic.

In the home of her employers, a battered and vicious Teatime makes a final appearance, demanding that Susan choose between saving her children and Death himself. Susan throws the nursery poker (which only kills monsters) through Death and into Teatime, killing him.

Once again, the finale behaves as if Susan was always the protagonist of the story, rather than someone helping out. If only the middle of the book felt the same way!

This pattern is repeated once again in *Thief of Time*. There's less focus on Death, who doesn't get much of a subplot to himself this time around, and this allows for more Susan page time. But not a lot more. The Auditors, the otherworldly creatures of Order who were behind Teatime's attack on the Hogfather, now attempt to stop time itself through the creation of a truly perfect glass clock out of a fairy tale.

The titular Thief of Time is a young orphan, Lobsang Ludd, who was raised by the Monks of History and turns out to be the illegitimate son of Time herself. He is taken on as an apprentice by Lu-Tze the Sweeper, who prepares him for a great quest, to stop the building of the clock and save history.

The master-apprentice relationship between the two men is smart and banterific, with all manner of hidden depths. Lu-Tze feels like an amalgam of a whole bunch of racial stereotypes, but he's still enjoyable on the page, with his subversive attitude towards heroics, violence and traditional masculinity. He feels at times like a male amalgam of Granny Weatherwax and Nanny Ogg—capable of great power, but most happy when people see nothing but a little old unthreatening person and underestimate him like whoa.

Lobsang's frustration with the master who won't apparently teach him anything (while sneakily teaching him all of the important things) mirrors Magrat and Agnes' respective journeys alongside the older witches of Lancre. As suggested by the title, the book is very much Lobsang's story, and the climax of the plot revolves around how he is able to utilise Lu-Tze's teachings.

> *'Most people call me Lu-Tze, lad. Or 'Sweeper'. Until they get to know me better, some call me 'Get out of the way'. I've never been very venerable, except in cases of bad spelling.'*

So where's Susan? Tidying up in the B plot, as usual. She is now a schoolteacher who uses all of her otherworldly abilities and innate practical ruthlessness to provide an unparalleled education for the children under her care. She has a life, in other words, and isn't pleased when summoned indirectly by her grandfather (he never asks in person, always sends the rat and the raven!) to interfere in a matter he himself is not allowed to be involved with.

Once again, Susan is absent for large sections of the book, while Lobsang is Learning Stuff and the Auditors themselves discover how hard it is to walk in human shape without their brains turning dangerously human too. Susan isn't given much to do (are you surprised? I'm not) until the final act, when time is stopped and everything goes pear-shaped.

Along with Lu-Tse and Lobsang, the other most interesting relationship in *Thief of Time* is between Susan and Myria/Unity LeJean, the Auditor who takes on human shape to commission the clock and is quickly seduced, damaged and infiltrated by the messiness of human nature. This is the closest thing we see to a female friendship for Susan since the schoolgirls from *Soul Music* (who didn't really know her that well), and it's an intense, complicated, utterly awkward combination of two people who both have to work hard at pretending to be human.

The use of chocolate and other foods as sensory weapons against the Auditors (who are intensely vulnerable to anything that smacks of humanity) and Unity's use of illogical signs to keep them at bay are nothing short of brilliant, and the 'boy talk' scene in which Unity embarrasses Susan with intimate questions and revelations about their respective attractions for Lobsang and his 'brother' (really the other half of him) Jeremy is greatly revealing of both of their characters.

While there are a couple of elements of the way Myria/Unity's character is handled that make me uncomfortable (mostly her self-diagnosis of being Completely Insane and how that meant she had to die, but also the whole gendered joke about women's relationship to chocolate) all her scenes are electric, and I appreciate how she and Susan work as a team.

Susan names Unity, insisting that its a better choice for her than Myria—being an individual rather than representing the many—and this is a deeply symbolic act that ties them together. I'm so sorry that the story ends with Unity's suicide, as I would have adored to see her embracing her new humanity (with Susan's help) rather than giving up on it.

Meanwhile, there's a sneaky romance. Yes, another one. Between Susan and Lobsang. Possibly. They hardly ever cross paths through the book, but that's the story of Susan's life. Her subtle relationship with Lobsang is handled exactly the same way as her interactions with Buddy and Bilious: their few scenes together involve them getting snarky at each other on early acquaintance and never quite managing to convey any mutual attraction. Susan's buried interest in Lobsang is noticed by other characters, but not something she ever admits to—the two of them have one or two angst-filled conversations, once it becomes obvious that he is going to have to leave humanity behind, but there is no overt romance until the very final scene of the book, which makes it clear through some very understated (DID I

MENTION SUBTLE) writing that Lobsang (maybe) returns Susan's (possible) feelings.

They're utterly repressed and not quite human—perfect for each other, in other words, but basically doomed as a couple. If there's ever another Susan book I fully expect that Lobsang will not be mentioned in it.

(Author's Note: there was not, in fact, another Susan book)

I was not expecting to be quite so critical of Susan's portrayal in the Discworld books—she's always been a character I liked (and still do like, very much) and I think she's a great example of how Pratchett improves radically in his portrayal of young female characters after his first five or ten books. It's such a shame that she is not allowed to be a protagonist through a whole book, instead of being introduced and then waiting patiently while everyone else gets the character development and plot bunnies out of the way, only to turn up with her scythe at the end to kick butt and take names.

Susan has grown up from book to book, and what we have of her is awesome. She is a powerful female character who balances domestic skills with battle skills, isn't distracted by romance, gets the job done every time and then returns to the life she has built for herself. She's extraordinary.

But I remain saddened she did get to pick up the scythe one more time, before Pratchett finally laid down his pen. It would have been nice to see her to take central stage for a whole book, in a plot that revolved around her: Susan Sto Helit, Granddaughter of Death. Protagonist.

8

POLE DANCERS, GOBLIN GIRLS, AND THE FAMILY MAN

Thud (2005)

Snuff (2011)

I KNOW I read *Thud* when it came out. But this was the early days of motherhood when my memory retention was out the window. I know I read this book, but it was a speedy, uninvolved reading. It had to be. Because there is no other excuse for me not realising before now that this is SO GOOD.

For a start, this is the best Angua novel since *Feet of Clay*—I think it might actually be better, in the attention given to her character. I like that she and Carrot have been allowed now to settle into a comfortable relationship. I also like that her main plotline for this novel is about her interactions with another female character.

Sybil also gets to shine in this book, despite her new motherhood.

Then there's Cheery, who doesn't get a subplot or even a subplotlet of her own, but remains awesome, and gets to play with the other girls.

There are two new women of note introduced in *Thud*. Salacia Delorisista Amanita Trigestrata Zeldana Malifee (etc.) von Humpeding, or Sally for short, is the first vampire that Vimes has allowed into the Watch. I was really pleased that Pratchett chose to do this plotline with a female character. Sally's personality provides an interesting contrast to the other female characters in and around the Watch and I thought it was a clever choice that, while she looks young, her age is cited as 50 (most fictional vampires tend to be much older or much younger than this). Her apparently effortless confidence could as easily be due to her age as her status as vampire.

Angua reacts badly to Sally. I was wary at first about the female jealousy trope being trotted out here, but Pratchett is at pains in the narrative to show that this is a natural werewolf reaction to a vampire, rather than anything gendered. Still, a lot of clichés about 'the new girl' trope flit through the story, particularly with Sally's attraction to Carrot.

Sally and Angua's uneasy partnership makes for great reading. Angua's is constantly interrogating how she feels about Sally, and internally questioning her own reactions from a gender point of view. Sally is as it turns out, neither a completely innocent sweetheart, nor a vixen out to steal Angua's man. I appreciate that Pratchett also shows us Carrot's attractiveness from Sally's point of view, the final hurdle of straight men trying to write the female gaze. Depicting female lust for a hot bloke is a rare thing in a) fantasy fiction by men and b) the Discworld in particular, so thumbs up for that one.

The other new female character we have, Tawneee, Nobby's pole dancer girlfriend, comes to the aid of the women in the Watch and consequently becomes far more integral to their story than Nobby's. When Sally takes Angua, Cheery and Tawneee on a girl's night out to thank Tawneee for her assistance, they get to know her as a person, and deal with the elephant in the room, which is basically how a strange little person like Nobby (whose bizarre appearance is really nothing compared to his bewildering personality) could attract such a hot girlfriend.

I'm wary of this subplot, because it relies on clichéd ideas that are very dated, and smack of "what men think women talk about when no men are present." I'm uncomfortable with how the girls were so quick to suggest that Tawneee could do better than Nobby based on her appearance. The main topic of their girls night out is the 'jerk' syndrome, whereby some women are so preternaturally attractive that no 'normal' man is likely to get up the nerve to ask them out, so only guys who are too dumb or 'jerky' to know the girl is out of their league will ask them out, and by that stage the girl is so lacking in self confidence that she'll take anyone.

Yeah. It's all a bit 90's sitcom, and I raised my eyebrows a lot through those scenes. Ultimately, though, the way that Tawneee and Nobby resolve their relationship makes me feel better about the plot, and it's nice to see the women of the Watch bonding so successfully.

Sybil, sadly, is not invited to the girl's night out, but that's understandable as she has a baby to deal with. The presence of Young Sam is used mostly for Vimes' character development, as happened in previous books; *Thud* in particular has a tight focus on Vimes' changing priorities now that he is a dad. I was irritated on Sybil's behalf that we see Vimes continuing to duck and weave his responsibilities as a husband, while being totally awesome about his responsibilities as a dad. On the other hand, once you have a baby that's the way around you'd choose to have it… but it's still uncomfortable. Sybil herself is the one who adapts, figuring out how to balance her husband's limited time and patience with her own needs, as shown at the end where she gives up on the idea of having him sit for a painted portrait and goes for a photograph instead.

Still, Vimes is an excellent dad, and the exploration of how he balances his workaholic ways with his commitment to reading The Story to his son at bedtime is emotionally compelling. Pratchett released a gorgeous picture book, *Where's My Cow?* that ties in with *Thud* and became my partner's official Daddy book to read to our eldest child for a good couple of years—it is all about the importance of reading to your kids every night, and sharing your world with them instead of some idealised picture book version of reality.

Sybil doesn't disappear completely into motherhood, thank goodness—her intelligence and insight is raised repeatedly through this story, and her own cultural interests prove to be useful to the plot—her knowledge of dwarf language comes up regularly, and her teenage fascination with art and geometry are vital to the resolution of the plot. She insists on joining Vimes on his journey at the end, not only because she wants to keep her family together, but also because she's not going to let him go off to Koom Valley on his own when it has been her own lifelong dream.

I love that Sybil sees herself as a robust woman. This comes up back in *The Fifth Elephant*, when she gives Vimes that lecture on how her family were bred to breed. Sadly this was somewhat dented in *Night Watch* when her robustness was sacrificed for a bit of narrative WOMAN IN LABOUR PANIC.

Here in *Thud*, when Sybil and her son come under attack, she is vulnerable but strong, and again cites the traditions of her family. Considering how often aristocratic women are portrayed in fantasy fiction as frail waifs who can barely survive a cold (as opposed to those rough, tough peasant women with babies on their backs) I enjoy it when Sybil cites her own family history as precedent for her own resilience, strength and general badassery.

When I first heard the title of the latest Pratchett novel, *Snuff*, I wondered if it might be the last. Sadly, as his health began to fail, the last few volumes of this series all carried that weight of 'what if this is the last one.'

It's a very good Sam Vimes novel, and takes his character to new places, something I wouldn't have thought possible. It is also, quite excellently, a good Sybil Vimes novel, and I was delighted to see that Vimes's love, desire and respect for his wife is articulated more clearly in this novel than previously, where his actions have mostly spoken for his feelings.

There is a sense of completion to Vimes' story with this book. His interactions with Feeney Upshot, the young local constable in the village of Ramkin Manor, are notably different to his previous mentoring narratives, because Upshot already has the right ideas in his head—he has read Vimes' speeches from afar. The character's legend has spread to the point that he isn't needed in person to make change in the world—and, as we see here, he's not even always the right man for the job. He can afford take a holiday. Even a policeman's holiday.

Once again, Vimes' developing relationship with his son Young Sam is front and centre in the story, with added bonus male bonding with Willikins the butler, a character who has developed dramatically since his first appearance, and whose loyal friendship with his 'master' is now essential to these stories.

Snuff does, however, give us little of the usual supporting characters—it offers an epilogue style resolution for Sgt Colon and Nobby, but hardly uses Cheery, Angua, Carrot or any other City Watch characters. Sally isn't mentioned. But then it's not, actually, a City Watch novel at all—it's a Vimes novel. Still, we've come a long way from the boy's own narrative of *Guards! Guards!* Apart from Sybil's splendid contributions, *Snuff* offers a wealth of varied and interesting female characters in supporting roles.

The plot of *Snuff* contains the signature beats of most Vimes novels from *Men At Arms* on: Vimes learns to overcome his prejudices about a particular type of person/creature and subsequently becomes their champion in the universe. In this case, it's goblins.

We meet Miss Beedle, a thinly veiled avatar of a certain Ms Rowling (with perhaps a side helping of Andy Griffiths) in our universe, an acclaimed children's author who has taught kids everywhere to be fascinated with poo. When not writing famous novels, she is secretly tutoring the daughter of the much-despised goblins in the ways of civilisation so that they can pass things on to their children and change the world.

The local toffs have their own smuggling operation, and as well as supplying deadly drugs for trolls, they are responsible for treating goblins as vermin and shipping them out of the village as slaves. While the son of recurring villain/antagonist Lord Rust is supposed to be the main villain of this group of aristocrats who believe they are above the law, it's actually the ruthless female magistrate 'Mrs Colonel' who comes across as the most compelling, creepy and entitled antagonist.

When Vimes discovers the awful treatment of the goblins, his first instinct is to deal with it through law: arresting people, upsetting the upper classes and generally causing havoc in his desperation to make the world bend to his newly found perspective on how *people* the goblins are. But while her husband is leaping around on riverboats, pursuing slavers and murderers, it's Sybil who actually goes about making effective change.

Discreetly, with letter-writing and gently persuasive words, Sybil stages a public event in Ankh-Morpork attended by aristocrats, culture lovers and ambassadors of all kinds, providing a showcase for the beautiful music played by Tears of the Mushroom, a young goblin woman. This creates more allies to their cause than any amount of Vimes telling people how wrong they are.

The combination of Sybil and Vimes is diabolical, and they will clearly continue to achieve great things in their marriage.

I also enjoyed, in *Snuff*, the "casual drive-by" female characters, who were so much interesting than the random sexy lamps I might trip over in the early Discworld novels. The gaggle of daughters waiting for husbands, to whom Vimes gives a lecture about finding a useful path in the world, could have represented an awful and patriarchal mansplaining situation, but this is mitigated by the fact that the girls' mother and Sybil orchestrated his presence precisely so that his plainspoken habits will put a bomb under the crinolines.

There is also a sly moment at the end where, Vimes having got rid of Lord Rust's corrupt son, Vetinari is not happy about the replacement heir Regina:

> *'Frankly, I was looking forward to dealing with the son, who is an ignorant, arrogant, pompous idiot, but his sister? She is smart!'*

Vetinari's ongoing (silent) battle with the lady who designs the crossword puzzles in the *Times* is also a nice touch. He is a character usually surrounded by other men (except the Aunt in *Night Watch* and the occasional moment when Lady Sybil decides to have a firm word with Havelock), so it's nice to see the Patrician deal with a female nemesis who is worthy of his respect.

I would have loved to read that novel.

9

THE TRUTH HAS GOT HER BOOTS ON

The Truth (2000)

I ALMOST WASN'T GOING to write a Pratchett's Women piece for *The Truth*. Like *Night Watch*, it's a marvellous book, but I never thought of it as one that had much to say about women or gender. *The Truth* is a love letter to moveable type, and a fun take on the history of the printing press, with the usual Discworld layers of humour and cleverness, and a rich cast of characters. It's easily forgiven it for the ensemble being so overwhelmingly male. This was the book that brought me back to the Discworld after losing interest somewhere in its middle years.

I wasn't alone in that. *The Truth* was a huge success for Terry Pratchett, and is one of the books that helped to cement his 'legend' status among mainstream readers as well as diehard fans. He had previously written other novels with a similar formula (standalone male character deals with the Discworld's crazy version of an industrial development borrowed from our own history, and chaos ensues) but there was something about this book, and its maturity, that made it special. This is also a story that features fewer overt fantasy elements than any previous Discworld novel—it's certainly not a story about magic gone wrong and trying to kill you, which sets it apart from the series. Instead, this is a story of PEOPLE gone wrong and trying to kill you, and how societal change can be every bit as terrifying and dangerous as anything from the Dungeon Dimensions.

Did I mention? This novel is magnificent.

On my reread I discovered that the story of William de Worde and *The Ankh-Morpork Times* is very much a story about gender issues, though William himself is unaware of it. *The Truth* is about the patriarchy, and how it hurts men every bit as much it hurts women. If I was writing a book about Pratchett's Men (and really, someone should, I would read the hell out of that book) I would discuss how traditional masculinity and other paternal themes are continually addressed and undercut in this story, which is very much about the Men Who Shape The World and the Legacy They Leave Behind. This continues the Discworld tradition of subverting narratives of masculinity—he's been doing this from page 1, book 1, with characters like Rincewind and Twoflower, Vetinari, Ridcully, Vimes, Moist Von Lipwig, Cohen the Barbarian and even some of the one-off 'heroes' like Pteppic, Buddy and Victor.

But this is not that book. So I'm going to talk about Sacharissa Cripslock.

Sacharissa is the only full-blooded female character in a sea of mostly invisible women (including the upwardly mobile wife and daughter of Harry King, William's sister, the dwarves who might not be male after all, a few absent mothers and so on). Mrs Arcanum the landlady and her Opinions represent an important ongoing subplot, though rather more attention in those scenes is given to Mr Windling and his Opinions—Mrs Arcanum is saved mostly for comic relief. Sgt Angua makes an important cameo appearance, though she looms larger in the books behind the scenes than actually on the page. There is a running joke based on William's belief that Nobby Nobbs is the rumoured werewolf in the City Watch, and the reader's presumed knowledge that in fact it is Angua. Sadly, as in the City Watch books, most of the interesting things Angua gets to do happen offpage.

But Sacharissa is pretty awesome. Apart from the running gag about her boobs (they are mighty and marvellous to behold, by all accounts) and the oft-quoted line about her face being 'eclectically attractive', she is very much part of the story because of her personality. Pratchett is at his most comfortable when writing intensely pragmatic women, and Sacharissa is very much in this vein. Her primary personality quirk at the beginning of the story is an obsession with historically ladylike behaviour, and what is 'seemly' for a lady to do, wear and say (which pretty much puts her on par with Mrs Arcanum). While William thinks such beliefs are frivolous and unnecessary, for Sacharissa they must be essential survival skills in a world that veers from medieval attitudes to Victoriana to modern and back again without even a moment's notice. After all, she lives in a city that still thinks calling prostitutes 'seamstresses' is highly amusing.

I highly enjoyed watching Sacharissa steal the novel from under William's feet. Their romance, if you can call it that, is one of those vague baffled courtships that Pratchett writes so well, in which both parties spend the whole time loudly thinking about everything except their attraction to each other, and dancing around the subject so subtly that you're not always sure that he *meant* you think it was a romance at all. But for the most part, Sacharissa isn't bothered about impressing William—instead, they both fall deeply and equally in love with the newspaper business.

This romance is a threeway.

While most scenes are written from William's point of view, and Sacharissa is largely presented to the reader through his eyes, we still see how her love affair with *The Ankh-Morpork Times* unfolds differently to his. She's the one who embraces many of the practical day-to-day details of the business, like why you report on meetings with lots of names in them, how to cover the ordinary parts of city life, and especially how to craft headlines. While William is figuring out from the ground up how to manage concepts like Freedom of the Press, and how to report on big, 'weighty' political issues, Sacharissa is working behind the scenes to figure out everything else you need to put in a newspaper so that it is more than a front page. He'd be lost without her, and it's nice that by the end he has acknowledged that fact.

She's not doing the grunt work for no recognition, either. While William struggles against some of the realities of the printing and news trade, Sacharissa is several steps ahead of him. Her competence is shown clearly, and while William resents Sacharissa using her attractiveness to gain news tidbits from eager young men, there is more to her methods. She starts out with the contacts and experience in the printing industry that William lacks—in fact she only joins the *Times* in the first place after coming over to complain about her father the printer being put out of business.

Now that I come to think of it I'm not entirely convinced that the novel needed William in it.

Sacharissa's character arc in *The Truth* comes to a climax with the resolution of another running gag, that of the hard-boiled thug Mr Tulip and his method of swearing (mostly saying '-ing' a lot without bothering to fill in the verb). William sends Sacharissa into a socially awkward situation, giving her the key to his family's townhouse and permission to raid his sister's wardrobe for a suitable dress to wear for a ball. This goes against Sacharissa's instincts about feminine respectability, and she is so busy trying to deal with the fact that she's burgling a house (it never occurred to him to go with her to make her 'borrowing' legitimate) that she ends up in a far more dangerous situation, taken hostage by two assassins.

It's here that the Lois Lane analogy, which has been strongly implied in her Girl Reporter role so far, looms larger. Being kidnapped by bad guys was an everyday occurrence for the sassy reporter of the *Daily Planet*, but Sacharissa doesn't have a pet superhero to rescue her—and so she throws caution and her last vestiges of 'respectability' to the wind in order to rescue herself, along with a healthy bout of yelling and swearing, which she finds rather cathartic.

After that, it's up to Sacharissa and William to save their mutual true love, the newspaper itself, from disaster...

I find Sacharissa a likeable, complicated and useful character in an excellent novel. But I'm not entirely sure what her character is supposed to represent. Is she a satire on a certain old fashioned kind of young lady who needs to loosen her corsets a bit? Is her character journey about worrying less about what people think of her? Is she a feminist character, or an example of why the women of the Discworld need organised feminism? Mostly I think she's far too busy doing her goddamned job to worry about such things.

When she turns up again in *Going Postal*, it is noted that she wears a wedding ring, but continues to call herself 'Miss Cripslock'. So there's one piece of evidence that she is embracing modernism.

If nothing else, Sacharissa is a great example of a practical woman in a fantasy novel who dresses sensibly and is excellent at her job. Which now I come to think about it, makes her a spectacularly important role model. While there hasn't yet been a movie or other media adaptation made of *The Truth* (which is a shame because it would be *brilliant*), Sacharissa's passing role in *Going Postal* means that she has been portrayed on the small screen by the comic actress Tamsin Greig. This makes her about 20 years older than she is portrayed in the books, but considering how briefly she appears that's hardly important. The essence of the character as a caller-of-bullshit in modest attire is definitely there.

Amazingly, on the original book cover, Josh Kirby managed to draw Sacharissa with at least as many clothes on as she is described as wearing in the book. I consider that a triumph of sorts, compared to his earlier work.

10

SOCKS, LIES, AND THE MONSTROUS REGIMENT

AUTHOR'S NOTE: This essay was written in 2014 for the first edition of this collection, and I'm keeping it mostly the same, but I think it's worth noting that this is a novel that digs deeply into gender essentialism and how gender and sex are not necessarily the same thing... without actually using a lot of the language choices that we would generally use today to discuss issues to do with, for example, trans and non-binary people.

Even in re-reading this essay for republication in 2018 I found myself fighting pronouns. We can't decide for ourselves as readers which characters are actually male despite the biological reveal that they are "female" in the story... except as fannish head-canons, of course, where the Disc is your shellfish of choice.

I feel it's incredibly valuable that we get to see how many of the characters in the book are still working through their personal thoughts about gender presentation, performance and identity right up to the end of the story. Gender is, for many, a process and a spectrum rather than an obvious choice or identity.

I will be fascinated to see how 'gender disguise' fiction tropes will change into the future as trans and non-binary identities become more commonly understood. Hopefully we'll get even more wonderful, crunchy popular fiction that explores this...

Despite its often extremely binary approach to gender, this is a book based on the premise that the world would be better in many ways if we stopped defining and limiting other people by gender preconceptions. Sadly, in 2018, this is even more necessary a message than it was when first published, fifteen years earlier.

Monstrous Regiment (2003).

> *Besides, she thought as she watched Wazzer drink, you only thought the world would be better if it was run by women if you didn't actually know many women.*

ALL DISCWORLD BOOKS are worth reading. Some are good, many are splendid, and a few are so close to the perfect novel that it's hard to justify calling them anything else.

I've been rereading a lot of these books over the few years, and *Monstrous Regiment* is hands down the best of them, including my other previous favourites such as *Night Watch* and *Lords and Ladies*.

This is a gorgeous, layered, crunchy, deeply emotional novel. I'm very impressed with it. This time around.

My big confession is: I didn't like *Monstrous Regiment* the first time I read it, when it was released back in 2003. So the rereading experience this time around involved a lot of prodding at my inner self to look at what went wrong then, and why I am so much more in love with the book now.

I don't have the excuse (as with my young adoration of Ginger and Ptraci) that it was my teenage self that took against this astoundingly feminist book. I was in my mid-twenties and (I thought) pretty clued in about the importance of women in fantasy.

I've pinned this down to two factors that turned 2003 me off *Monstrous Regiment*:

1. The novel's trick of repeatedly pulling the rug out from under the reader (which is in fact the best thing about the novel and an essential aspect of its structure) by making gender reveal after gender reveal. This annoyed the hell out of me the first time around.
2. I really wanted Maladict to stay a male character, and was unbelievably cross that he turned out to be a girl. Possibly this is because I was shipping him with Polly.
3. A disappointing lack of male allies.

Having established in my previous *Pratchett's Women* essays that my teenage self was extremely shallow (not to mention heteronormative!), it's confronting to realise that my 25 year old self was almost as bad. Oh dear, me.

Monstrous Regiment almost does not need to be a Discworld novel. The first clue to this is in the creation of Borogravia, a country completely removed from the rest of the Discworld society and history, in order to create the conditions necessary for the novel to work. Yes, we have a touch of Vimes, but his role and that of his City Watch off-siders is little more than an extended cameo.

This is a war novel, and a very specific one, because it is a war novel about women who dress up as boys to go to the front line. The main character, Polly, makes this choice for herself and then goes to elaborate lengths to change her identity and sign up, only to slowly discover that the majority of the new volunteers in her platoon (with varying degrees of authenticity) have done the same thing.

It sounds like a gimmick, and to some extent it is, and yet it is a glorious gimmick because it allows Pratchett to take a story that has been written so many times before (*Monstrous Regiment* is an amalgam of every 'young man goes to war' story ever told) and tell it about women.

This is important because women are often left out of the narrative of war stories, except as the girl/wife/sister/daughter who keeps the home fires burning. *Monstrous Regiment* takes as its basic premise the idea that sending girls off to fight a war is no more abhorrent than doing so to teenage, untried boys (one of our more romanticised cultural myths), and that going into the grim realities of a battlefield is not necessarily the most dangerous fate for young women in a misogynist society.

Not content with subverting one extremely gendered narrative trope, Pratchett also takes the popular 'girl dresses as a boy in order to achieve a life goal in a sexist society' narrative tradition and subverts that too, especially the part where the girl protagonist in such books rarely spends any time building connections with other women.

If Polly had been the only one disguised as a boy in this story, there would have been no point in telling it.

Like our own modern culture, the Discworld has its share of sexism and gender essentialism, but not to such a heightened degree as was necessary for this story to work. Borogravia, then, is designed to be such an appalling place for women to live, that it makes Lancre look like a feminist Disneyland.

Polly's choice to go into the army is about survival rather than heroism. The only way to save her family tavern (and to keep running it as she always intended to) is to have a living brother to inherit it from their father — but, unfortunately, her brother has marched off to the sound of the army's drum, living status unknown. 'The Duchess' is a symbol of the life she knows, the name of the tavern she is fighting to protect as well as the name of Borogravia's supposed head of state, a quasi-deity who has not been seen in many years and is rumoured to be dead. To join the army, you kiss the Duchess (a coin with her head on it) as a form of oath, and Polly sideswipes her own inauthenticity by believing really hard in her own 'Duchess'.

> *Forget you were ever Polly. Think young male, that was the thing. Fart loudly and with self-satisfaction at a job well done, move like a puppet that'd had a couple of random strings cut, never hug anyone and, if you meet a friend, punch them.*

Some of the most entertaining sequences in the first half of the book are about Polly's mimicry of the young male of the species, based on observations from her life as a barmaid. She's remarkably good at it, to the point that the first time she 'disguises herself as a girl' by taking off her armour in a village under attack by the enemy, she feels a great sense of embarrassment and shame at being caught in a petticoat. This, of course, is foreshadowing.

The other girls she discovers in her platoon have different reasons for being there. Shufti is trying to find her 'husband' before her pregnancy becomes too obvious. Tonker and Lofty are escaping the dour and grim life of the Girls' Working School where 'bad girls' are sent. And Wazzer, who hears the voice of the (probably dead) Duchess in her head, is almost certainly Joan of Arc.

The story about the hapless team of new recruits, and their gradual discovery that the others are all girls, takes on a farcical element when even the troll and the 'Igor' are revealed to be female. Why should it matter that a large animate pile of rocks is male or female, or that a living jigsaw of borrowed limbs is an Igorina? It doesn't...except of course that it matters in how those characters are perceived, and whether they are taken seriously. Even a race with almost no physical differences between genders feels differently about men than it does about women.

The message of *Monstrous Regiment* is that gender is often thought to be important under circumstances where it should be irrelevant. Polly is a more capable person to run a tavern than her brother, but is held back because of her gender. Igorina has to hide her gender simply to be allowed to use her medical expertise in the field.

Carborundum/Jade chooses to grow lichen on her head to mask her gender, but this means overcoming her cultural association of baldness with feminine modesty. Polly cuts her hair off for the same reason, but can't quite bear to leave her ringlets behind and ends up in danger of discovery when a 'political' (spy within the army) steals the hair. Igorina goes a step further than any of them, sewing false stitches into her face to appear male as well as faking a lisp.

Thanks to her serious attention to detail in mimicking the body language of young men, Polly is one of the last of the group to be recognised as female by the others, and has to actually own up to it. The narrative goes into great detail about how she walks, speaks, pees standing up and so on, as well as the many ways she corrects and observes along the way.

Of course, Polly has been spotted right from the start, by the only person in the outfit who is a better observer than she is, and anonymously passes on the tip about the extra pair of socks she needs to stuff down the front of her trousers. What follows is possibly one of the most overworked and yet cleverly expressed metaphors of the history of the Discworld. 'Socks' to Polly becomes a metaphor for more than just a fake bulge, but also for masculinity and male behaviour as a whole.

> 'There is a difference,' said Shufti. 'I think it's the socks. It's like they pull you forward all the time. It's like the whole world spins around your socks.'

Finally, the disguise has to be laid aside in the name of strategy—Polly and the other girls take off their uniforms to 'pretend' to be women and infiltrate the enemy base as potential servants and laundresses. They are caught instantly as obvious soldiers in disguise, and only pass muster once one of them shows the physical evidence that she is female and pregnant.

Being in female clothes again deals a massive blow to Polly's identity. She is crawling up the walls to get back into her uniform even after the plot has unravelled, the day has been saved, and her gender has been revealed to everyone. She needs her socks back, and feels naked without them.

In a time of war, with their country on the brink of destruction, Polly and the other recruits bring down an enemy stronghold and rescue the remains of the (male) army. But in the process, they are unmasked as female. Despite their heroic achievements, the women face grave punishment for the crime of disguising themselves as men.

Sgt Jackrum, the gruff and shouty leader of "men", has been such a prominent figure in the story so far, not only teaching the young recruits about how to survive but proving to be a supportive ally even after he learns about their gender. He calls a closed court, demanding a certain number of generals and other high-ranked persons stay while others leave. At which point, he reveals that approximately one third of the current army, including everyone in the room, are women pretending to be men.

It's an absurdity, but this revelation is important because it says so much about their society. For the women in question, the shock is mostly that they did not know about each other. They all thought that their secret was unique.

The narrative still has more reveals to come—the rather anti-climactic confirmation that Maladict is female like the rest of the group, and the far more earth-shattering final uncovering of the truth about Sgt Jackrum himself.

Jackrum's reveal comes as a shock, even knowing that it was coming—though on a reread it becomes obvious how many clues are hidden in plain sight, such as his saying 'On my oath, I am not a violent man' as a regular catchphrase shortly before being very violent indeed. His declaration that the recruits are 'his little lads' and insistence on referring to them as such feels similarly like a vocabulary trick he is playing on the world.

Does Jackrum's reveal as a woman dent his status as a magnificent ally for the women under his command? Is his grand gesture in support of these young women less impressive once you know that he is a she? I thought so the first time around—certainly that was a big part of my frustration with this novel back in 2003. The tale of an old woman in disguise who helps other young women with their disguises felt less brave and heroic to me than if Jackrum was male.

Likewise, is Mal's calm acceptance of the women fighting at his side suddenly a whole lot less impressive once he is (belatedly) revealed to be Maladicta?

With both Maladicta and Jackrum (and even the suspiciously supportive defence lawyer) finally revealed as female, the only Borogravian ally to the women who is physically male is Lt Blouse. This young aristocratic officer qualifies for his position in all the ways that the army thinks matters, but is patently less cut out for war than most of the female recruits—though his amateur dramatics skills do come in rather handy. Having been useless in a military sense for most of the book, he comes into his own when he learns the truth about the female recruits, and unquestioningly gives them his support.

But does Lt Blouse's gender make him a better ally than Mal

or Jackrum? When I first read the book, I believed this to be the case, and I felt that the Maladict and Jackrum reveals (as well as that of the lawyer) were tacked on rather than significant. I hit a wall with the story as a younger reader because it felt like their gender reveal rendered their support null and void—not to mention sneaky and selfish rather than heroic.

I was wrong.

Men who publicly support feminism or issues that affect mostly women are regularly lauded as heroes for saying exactly the same thing that women have been saying for years. Even though it is an act of humanity, not masculinity, to make that stand.

Also, women are *not* always the best allies for other women, especially women in power who have struggled to get where they are. Glass ceiling, baby, that's what it's all about. Good female allies need to be appreciated because it's not by any means guaranteed that a woman will support you rather than throw you under the bus.

There are assholes everywhere, and cowards everywhere. Being brave on someone else's behalf is not a selfish act, regardless of gender.

Monstrous Regiment is a story about women. Women and women and women. And while I want to roll my eyes at my younger self for going through that reaction Jackrum's gender, I also think that experience is part of the intended reader experience—those questions are, I believe, exactly what Pratchett wants us to be asking ourselves.

Jackrum is the only person in power who chooses to help Polly and her recruits with their gendered issues, both before and after they have been outed as female. The same is true of all the other women she has recognised and helped over the years—and those dozens of female generals she confronts in the courtroom could have done the same thing BUT CHOSE NOT TO. *Monstrous Regiment* is not a story about men supporting women in their quest to be soldiers and fight for their country, it is a story about whether other women will support those women.

In *Monstrous Regiment*, as in the real world, often they don't.

Jackrum's violent and passionate public support of the young female recruits is awesome regardless of whether he is a man or she is a woman. If anything, the fact that she is a woman makes her stance braver because of the risk that she herself will be outed—and it's rather fascinating that she does not out herself in the courtroom even when surrounded only by women, almost as if she has forgotten that she is one of them.

Indeed, after winning the legal battle on behalf of her little lads, it's Sgt Major Jackrum herself who needs to be rescued from gender preconceptions—they have been avoiding retirement because there is nothing waiting for them in their civilian life after the army. They feel they can never reclaim their son and grandchildren because after living their whole professional life as an army man, they would only ever be an embarrassment to their family.

Polly is able to pay back some of Jackrum's support by giving her a new way of looking at the dilemma—retirement from the army doesn't mean she has to give up her male identity unless she chooses to do so. She can as easily turn up as a long lost dad and granddad to reclaim her family…

And indeed, when the 'iconograph' arrives to show Polly that Jackrum did indeed choose reclaim that lost family, it's left ambiguous as to whether they to live out their days as a Grandpa or Grandma. Ultimately, it's not something we need to know—surrendering to civilian life is Jackrum's great final quest, and their gender identity is none of our business.

> *'I... expected better of 'em, really. I thought they'd be better at it than men. Trouble was, they were better than men at being like men. They do say the army can make a man of you, eh? So... whatever it is you are going to do next, do it as you. Good or bad, do it as you. Too many lies and there's no truth to go back to.'*

Sgt Major Jackrum, advice to a young soldier upon retirement.

POLLY'S own happy ending is that she gets everything she wanted—her brother safe and alive, and The Duchess restored to their family. The addition of Shufti and her baby to the tavern even means she has a sensible female friend to help out around the house.

But then the war stirs again, and soldiers are needed.

I am reminded at this point of one of the great gender-switching fantasy series of all time, Tamora Pierce's *Lioness Quartet*. Alanna hides her gender throughout her whole training to become a knight, intending to tell the truth once she is Sir Alan/Alanna and then to go into self-imposed exile, not expecting anyone to forgive her for her deceit. After her true nature is revealed, and her sympathetic friend Jonathan takes his father's throne, he declares that women can legally train to be knights, forever into the future. But, they don't, for a whole decade, until one girl (in a later series by Pierce, The Protector of the Small) is brave enough to try —and her journey is much harder than Alanna's ever was.

Polly is in a similar situation—she is technically allowed to go into the army under a female identity this time around, but is not sure she is welcome.

> *We weren't soldiers, she decided. We were girls in uniform. We were like a lucky charm. We were mascots. We weren't real, we were always a symbol of something. We'd done very well, for women. And we were temporary.*

As SHE GEARS up to fight the war her own way, Polly looks at the uniforms that were provided once it was officially declared that the women soldiers were heroes instead of criminals: long skirts and bum rolls, plumes that make them look like dolls. She puts the skirt on, because sometimes it's useful to not look threatening, but she wears her trousers underneath.

Clothes matter. Anyone who thinks clothes are frivolous and irrelevant has simply not thought about the real effect they can have on people who are vulnerable because of their gender, or class, or other lack of privilege.

Polly sets off to stop a war, in the end, wearing trousers and a skirt. Maladicta joins her, and there are new recruits, too, who don't have to repeat history by pretending to be something they're not—unless they want to.

'Oh, you can join as men if you want,' said Polly. 'We need a few good men.'

The girls looked at one another.

'You get better swear words,' said Polly. And the trousers are useful. But it's your choice.'

A CHOICE like that is something worth fighting for.

ALSO BY TANSY RAYNER ROBERTS

BELLADONNA UNIVERSITY

Fake Geek Girl

Unmagical Boy Story

The Bromancers

MOCKLORE

The Mocklore Omnibus

Ink Black Magic

Bounty

MUSKETEERS IN SPACE

Musketeer Space

Joyeux

SHORT FICTION:

Love and Romanpunk

SUPERHEROES:

Kid Dark Against The Machine

Girl Reporter

CASTLE CHARMING

Glass Slipper Scandal

Dance, Princes, Dance

NON-FICTION & ESSAYS

It's Raining Musketeers

Pratchett's Women

SHEEP MIGHT FLY

LISTEN
to fun, magical stories read by award-winning SFF author Tansy Rayner Roberts

FREE EVERY WEEK
Sheep Might Fly
sheepmightfly.podbean.com

LOVE & ROMANPUNK

Thousands of years ago, Julia Agrippina wrote the true history of her family, the Caesars. The document was lost, or destroyed, almost immediately. (It included more monsters than you might think.)

Hundreds of years ago, Fanny and Mary ran away from London with a debauched poet and his sister. (If it was the poet you are thinking of, the story would have ended far more happily, and with fewer people having their throats bitten out.)

Sometime in the near future, a community will live in a replica Roman city built in the Australian bush. It's a sight to behold. (Shame about the manticores.)

Further in the future, the last man who guards the secret history of the world will discover that the past has a way of coming around to bite you. (He didn't even know she had a thing for pointy teeth.)

The world is in greater danger than you ever suspected. Women named Julia are stronger than they appear. Don't let your little brother make out with silver-eyed blondes. Immortal heroes really don't fancy teenage girls. When love dies, there's still opera.

Family is everything.

Monsters are everywhere.

Yes, you do have to wear the damned toga.

History is not what you think it is.

***Love & Romanpunk*, a short story collection.**

Available from Twelfth Planet Press.

Praise for Love & Romanpunk:

*"I was absolutely stunned by **Love and Romanpunk**. I expected quality. I did not expect revolutionary brilliance..."*

Seanan McGuire

"A series of interlinked short stories featuring the descendants of the Caesars, there's monster-killing, whimsy and a real dark heart to the book..."

Trent Jamieson

The same dry wit runs through all of the stories, and the plots have a little in common with gorgon hair: they twist around and can bite you unexpectedly.

Cheryl Morgan

*"The obvious comparison for Rayner Roberts' work here is Buffy the Vampire Slayer. They both have vampires, slayers, and meaty relationships. But **Love and Romanpunk** is its own, self-contained vision, one that turns the wit and heart up as much as any story could sustain. Rayner Roberts' lean prose draws you in from the first few paragraphs and keeps that pace going straight through."*

Locus Magazine

This book was first published as a series of articles on http://tansyrr.com in 2011/2012

"Socks, Lies & the Monstrous Regiment" (2014) is original to this collection

This collection © Tansy Rayner Roberts
(2014, 2018)

First Edition published by Fablecroft 2014
Second Edition published by the author 2018

This ebook is licensed for your personal enjoyment only. This ebook may not be re-sold or given away to other people. If you would like to share this book with another person, please purchase an additional copy for each reader. If you're reading this book and did not purchase it, or it was not purchased for your use only, then please return to your favorite retailer and purchase your own copy. Thank you for respecting the hard work of this author.

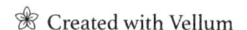

❦ Created with Vellum

Made in the USA
Las Vegas, NV
19 December 2021